TEAGAN: COWBOY STRONG

THE KAVANAGH BROTHERS BOOK ONE

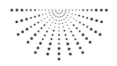

KATHLEEN BALL

CHAPTER ONE

*T*eagan Kavanagh pushed his hat back and frowned as he stared out over his pasture, dotted with grazing livestock. He shook his head and looked again. A good many of the cattle on his land didn't belong to him. "Tarnation!" he muttered as the truth dawned on him. Someone had knocked down the fence again.

Running his gaze over the fence in the distance, it didn't take him long to spot the breach. It was hard not to see considering several scrawny cows were jumping over the downed posts and wire and roaming onto his land as he watched. Still mumbling under his breath, he spurred his dun, Sandy through the hole in the fence and rode for the Maguire house.

The broken steps, unpatched roof, and the door barely hanging on its hinges surprised him. Why was the place in such disrepair? It couldn't cost that much to fix it up. They had plenty of cattle. Maybe they didn't know that because they were all on his land grazing on his grass.

The squawking of the chickens was the only sign that

anything alive was around. The ground was nothing but patches of dirt that blew like dust in the scorching Texas sun.

Teagan swung down off his horse, by-passed the porch steps and knocked on the house instead of the door. He waited, but nothing happened. No one answered. He hopped off the porch and went around back. The garden that had once been lush and vibrant with vegetables was no longer anything but a patch of weeds. But laundry on the clothesline was whipping in the wind. Someone lived here.

Then he saw her, Gemma Maguire. She was pulling with what seemed to be all her might on a rope around their old cow. It always was a stubborn animal, and time hadn't mellowed her one bit. He strode over and, without so much as a word of greeting, took the rope out of Gemma's hand, and with a firm tug to get her moving, he led Old Bennie into the falling-down barn and to her stall. He removed the rope and closed the stall door behind him when he was done.

When he turned around and walked out of the barn, she was waiting for him just outside the door.

"Gemma," he said in a neutral tone as he tipped his hat to her.

"Teagan. I heard all the boys made it home from the war. What a blessing." She quickly stared at the ground and shuffled her feet a bit. "I guess you want to evict me. I'm trying to locate any family I might have, plus the bank said I still had one month before I had to either pay off the loan or leave." Her chin wavered, and she swallowed hard. "I… suppose you could say I've hit on hard times."

"Where are your folks?"

"Mama died of consumption, and Daddy never did come back from the war. I married a man who promised to take care of the ranch and me, but he took all my money and left. I guess I wasn't very good at picking a husband. He tried to sell the land right from under me but there was too much debt, all his debt. He liked to play cards at Bobbie's Saloon for days at a time." She stole a quick look at him and bowed her head again. "I will pack."

"I didn't buy your ranch, Gemma."

She narrowed her eyes as she stared at him. "Of course, you did. Mr. Lyons told me how you wanted me gone right away but he worked it out so I could stay until the end of the month. He said Teagan Kavanagh bought the place with cash."

He shook his head, trying to make sense of her words. "I don't understand any of this. When's the last time you had a good meal?"

She turned crimson. "It's not important."

He touched her arm and was struck by a jolt of awareness; he still felt a spark between them after all this time. "It is important. I hate to say this Gemma, but you look worse than the beggars in the city."

Stepping away, she turned her back on him. "I will be out by the end of the month." Gemma lifted her skirt a bit and ran to the house. She almost fell on the busted-up steps, and she was extremely gentle with the door.

They had once been such good friends. Good friends until he'd asked her to marry him, at least... and she said no. He hadn't even been aware she got married. He supposed he had never really known her at all. His hands fisted as he walked to Sandy then swung up into the saddle.

A wry chuckle bubbled forth. He never had gotten to the reason he'd come over; the cattle.

As he rode, he couldn't help but compare the worn-down woman he'd just left to the vital young lady she'd once been. Her blossom of youth had vanished, her hair looked uncombed, and her dress has seen better days. *I married a man who promised to take care of the ranch and me..."* Her words echoed in his head, and he couldn't get the broken look she'd worn as she told him out of his mind. *She married someone else*. The notion was pure torture and would not leave him alone while he rode through his herd and got a better sense of how many head she had on his property.

Heading home and asking his brothers a few questions might clear things up. Then he would see Victor Lyons and find out why Gemma thought he was buying her ranch.

***

SHE HADN'T SET eyes on him for at least six years. He'd grown up, hardened some, but mostly he was the same. She'd fallen for him the minute she first saw him with his broad shoulders, sky-blue eyes, and brown hair. He'd been confident bordering on arrogance back then. He seemed more reserved now. She'd spent far too much time crying over that man.

Her father had hated the whole Kavanagh family, and he'd forbidden her to marry Teagan. In fact, the day Teagan had asked her, she had been ordered to tell him he'd be shot on sight if he came near her again. The confusion and hurt in his eyes had haunted her all these years. When the Kavanagh boys joined up to fight the war, she'd been terrified he'd be killed.

At first, she had ridden the fence line between their ranches to glean a bit of information about how he was doing, but none of the brothers would talk to her. Losing their friendship had cut deep, but she didn't have a choice. Her father never told her why he hated Mr. Kavanagh.

She prayed so much for the boys in gray. Then her father had joined the army and soon after that, her mother had died. What a terrible time it was. Few folks helped her, and she had never understood why. Her mother had been friendly to them all.

Then the soldiers had raided her food. She dug a new

root cellar, but it was discovered, and the army took her food. Finally, she walked a good half hour and dug another new one. She planted her garden out there too, after the one near her house had been raided to the extent there was nothing left. She'd been lucky she'd had enough time to grow and harvest again.

She'd picked all the wild berries she could find and made preserves. It was a long trek in the winter, and she spent much of the time covering her tracks. It was a lonely time, and though they were her nearest neighbors, not one of the Kavanaghs had checked on her. She paid the mortgage every month with money she'd found buried in her yard. Her father hadn't trusted banks. As far as she'd known everything had been paid off.

It had proven a struggle, but she had been getting by. One day after church, a handsome man with blond hair and brown eyes had smiled at her. He'd asked her to go for a walk. He was funny and charming. His manners were polished, and he was so respectful. The other unmarried women in the town all had their eyes on him, but every Sunday he'd chosen her. She'd been too smitten by his attentions to realize she was just being played for a fool.

Shoving the memories aside, she stared out the window and into her ruined garden. If Teagan didn't know about the land buy, then what was going on? It was time—past time,—for answers. She'd need to draw a hot bath and press her Sunday dress, for tomorrow she was going to the Kavanagh's.

IT WAS a bit of a walk to the Kavanagh's house; a dry, hot, sweaty walk. Hopefully her shoes would hold together. She could see the house and outbuildings from a distance, and the difference between the state of their house and hers shamed her. The Kavanagh house was beautifully white-washed, and she had always admired the big porch. A person could walk out any door of the house and be on the porch. Their steps looked to be in fine condition, and she'd bet they didn't have water leaking into the house when it rained. To think her house had once been in such fine order as that.

A sigh slipped past her lips, and she squared her shoulders. She'd done the best she could, and she'd survived. She had made some bad, life-altering decisions, but here she was. Which of the boys would answer the door? Or did they still have Dolly working for them? She had checked the notices of death constantly and she had never seen the name Kavanagh on any of them, but the notices weren't always correct.

She stood very straight and tall and hesitated. Teagan wouldn't want to see her. She'd lost her pride when she told him about her life. What had she been thinking? A hush seemed to settle around her. No birdsong, no chirp and hum of insects. No voices. No one was around. She should turn around and leave…

The door swung inward, and the Kavanagh's housekeeper stood framed in the opening. "Mrs. Parks," Dolly greeted. "I saw you walk up, but I didn't hear you knock. Well, come on in. I haven't seen you in a while not since… Well, it's been a while."

Gemma walked in. "It's good to see you too, Dolly." Gemma had always admired the woman who had practically raised the boys. Dolly had black hair she wore braided. It hung down her back and was as thick as a man's wrist. She was older and she ruled the house with an iron hand. It was as though she was the conscience of the household. The boys had often looked to her for advice.

"I was just making some tea. Would you care to join me?" Dolly tilted her head slightly, and her smile was welcoming, but not as warm as normal, as though she knew this wasn't a social call.

"That sounds lovely. Is Teagan available? I need to talk to him."

Dolly shook her head. "He grumbled about bankers and went to town."

Gemma's heart quickened. So, he knew about the sale. She gave a nod. "The tea sounds good if you're still offering."

"Of course. Please have a seat, and I'll be right back."

Dolly walked to the kitchen, and with each step she took, Gemma lost a bit more of her confidence. Dolly had such poise and manners. Gemma felt like a country hick compared to her. She sat in a comfortable chair facing the lavish stone fireplace that took up half the wall. It was beautiful when lit during a frigid day. At least that was how she remembered it.

Was Teagan chastising the banker for telling her who had bought the land? Did she have any prayer of paying him off? Would he help her? She must have a few stray cattle somewhere, but without a horse to round them up, she couldn't claim them as collateral against any debt. No, she'd drink her tea as quickly as she could while still being polite and then she was leaving. Coming here was just another bad decision to add to her long list.

Dolly returned with a tray that held the tea and sugar cookies to have with it. Gemma's mouth watered as she stared at those cookies. Dolly poured a cup of tea and handed it over. "If I remember you like it plain?"

"Yes, thank you." Gemma waited for Dolly to be seated before she took a sip. It was heavenly. She hadn't had tea in a while, so she savored each sip. The sugar cookie had extra sugar sprinkled on top. It had been a long while since she'd had sugar.

"Oh, Teagan is back," Dolly announced as she hopped up and opened the door for him. "You have a visitor."

Teagan glanced at her and didn't bother to hide his scowl. "Miss. Maguire, please come with me to my office."

"Mrs. Parks," Dolly corrected.

Gemma stood. Her face heated. "It's still Maguire. My husband already had a wife when he married me." Shamed, she walked to the office, now Teagan's office. It still looked and smelled the same. Everything was made of leather and there was still a hint of the scent of his father's pipe tobacco in the air.

Teagan caught up and closed the door. "Please have a seat."

She remained standing. "Dolly told me you went to see Mr. Lyons?" she pressed. No sense stalling, she decided as she met his gaze.

Teagan took his time getting settled behind the massive wooden desk. "What we have is a bit of a mystery. Mr. Lyons didn't have any signed papers from a buyer. Interestingly enough, you are not behind on your payments, so I don't understand why he told you to leave at the end of the month. At first, he pretended to not know what I was talking about. He was lying. He's still lying, but now he can't hold anything over you. I took the liberty of paying off your debt, and the house and land are yours."

"You—*what?*" Why would he do something like that? And how...? She forced her racing mind to slow down so she could have a civil conversation with him. "I'll pay you back every cent." She would just have to figure out how. "I-I can't even pretend to know what is going on." She sank down on one of the leather chairs. "I had the land and everything all paid for. It took a lot of going without, but I didn't mind. I didn't want anyone to think they could take it after the war. But then... Well, my husband..." She wrung her hands. "I'll pay you the first of the month." She stood and turned toward the door.

"Wait! How do you expect to pay me?"

"Well… I must have some cattle… somewhere."

He gave a curt nod. "You do, currently grazing on my land. How do you expect to round them up? You don't have a horse, do you?"

"Just how many cattle are we talking about? I figured I had a few hiding in a canyon or something."

He was going to tell her to get off the property. Saying that she had no business running a ranch.

"I'm sorry your first husband didn't work out," Teagan said gently. "But you need help. I'll figure out which of my brothers will marry you."

The breath left her lungs in a whoosh. "You will *what?* Listen *Mr.* Kavanagh, you may be able to tell people on this ranch what to do, but I'm not one of them." She gave him a hard, angry stare. Arrange for her to marry one of his brothers? How absurd!

"Where do you plan to go?"

"It's none of your business."

"Yes, it is. All right, I lied. I paid it off, and I hold the note on the property. The only way I'm getting paid back is if you have a husband to rebuild the ranch."

"You take too much upon yourself. I will never marry again."

"Is there one brother over another you'd prefer?" He sat back and crossed his arms.

Her heart jumped. The fight went out of her momentarily as she stared into his eyes. Yes, there was, but he'd never believe her. "I won't subject any of your brothers to a loveless marriage."

"Is that what you had, a loveless marriage?" His voice turned taunting.

"Yes, if you must know. I settled and I knew it, but I didn't know just how hard it could be. The man I really loved was always on my mind, and Richard was well aware who that was. He threw it in my face every chance he got. He spent more time at Bobbie's Saloon than he did at home, and he wasn't always gambling. People whispered about it every time I was in town." She heaved a sigh. "But that was my burden to bear. I refuse to marry again. I had my heart torn out once, and I won't do it again." She opened the door and walked out of the office.

Just who did he think he was? *"You don't have a horse, do you?"* he'd said, as if that would solve all her problems. Well, she had two good feet; she'd drag her cattle back. A soft snarl curled her lip as she thought about her cattle on Kavanagh land. That no-good banker had led her to believe they'd been rustled. She knew the Kavanaghs weren't thieves. She walked and walked, aware that her shoes were rubbing her feet raw, limping more with each painful step.

The door to the house was off its hinges and on the ground. Had someone been there? Did she dare check inside? She grabbed the axe off the chopping stump and walked to the door then cautiously pushed it open. No one was there. In fact, nothing was there; all her things had been taken, furniture and all. What was going on? She'd had to be strong for so long... And now she not only didn't have a horse, she had nothing. Great gasping sobs tore through her body.

She sat on the porch and cried.

CHAPTER TWO

*A*s Teagan paced the small room he used as an office, his thoughts strayed—as they typically did in the last couple of days—to Gemma Maguire Parker? No, she'd said her marriage wasn't legal and she was still Maguire. Maybe she was right about her not marrying. He could understand why she wouldn't want to tie herself to anyone again. But she couldn't keep one of his brothers from working the ranch. He could sleep in the barn... No that would have tongues wagging. His brother could simply come home every night and sleep.

He would do whatever it took to make sure she was safe and had a roof over her head. Why was she always so stubborn? She'd been just as cantankerous when he'd proposed to her; refusing to even explain why she'd said no. The man she mentioned loving... he hadn't so much as suspected she cared about someone, but the unnamed man must have been why she turned down his proposal. Teagan shook his head. He had to stop thinking of that. But the heartache and wondering had never gone away.

Teagan opened the office window, letting in a wisp of

breeze. Quinn should be here soon. He'd do a good job and there would be no worries about them getting together; Quinn didn't trust women. He'd keep an eye on all the hands he took with him. It was the perfect solution.

"Quinn, I was just thinking about you." Seating himself behind the desk, Teagan smiled at his brother. Quinn was taller than Teagan and thinner; he was faster too. But they'd both been cut from the same basic pattern. They both had brown hair with sky-blue eyes. They had constantly been called by each other's names when they were young. Now, though, Quinn hardly smiled.

"Think fast. I have a lot to do today." He plopped down on the leather couch.

A frown pinched Teagan's brow as he took in the distance between couch and desk. It really wasn't close enough to the couch for a conversation. Quinn had probably chosen that seat on purpose. Teagan moved to one chair near the couch.

"We have a bit of a problem. Gemma is living by herself, and her house is falling down around her. Apparently, she married a con man who bilked her out of all her money plus took out a loan on the land. He was already married to someone else at the time he married her and neglected to let her know that little fact." He suppressed a wince, just thinking about Gemma married to someone, especially someone who had abused her trust, pained him. He shook his head to dispel the mood. "I paid off the loan and now hold the note. I don't want to be paid back, but she doesn't know that. I want her ranch turned successful again." He rubbed his jaw with one hand as his mind started putting a plan together. "She has more than enough cattle on our land to make a go of it. We all know she doesn't want me over there, so I'm sending you. If you need more help take or hire some, but they sleep here at night. She's not feeding anyone either. I'm not positive she's feeding herself."

Quinn stared at him without blinking. "You want me to what? I'm supposed to babysit the woman you still love and make her life livable?"

Teagan gave a curt nod. "That sounds about right. I thought you could go first thing in the morning and help her plan how she'd like her place set up. She'd be better off if we just tore the whole place down and started over, but she has her pride." He snapped his fingers as another thought occurred to him. "Also, we need to loan her a horse. She seemed surprised when I told her that her cattle were on our land. I don't believe she thought she had cattle anymore."

Quinn sighed and shook his head, obviously coming around to the idea. "Poor kid, she's had it hard. He didn't hit her, did he?"

Teagan's frown returned. "I didn't think to ask. I know he spent his nights with those soiled doves of Bobbie's."

"Her cattle have been on our land for a long while. I never had the fence fixed, hoping they'd go home." He angled his head and studied Teagan. "Parents dead?"

"Yes, and I don't think she has anyone else."

Quinn ran his fingers through his hair. "I'll do it… only because she's always been kind to me. Plus, I know she's your woman so there won't be any complications."

Teagan didn't bother to correct Quinn of the notion that Gemma was his woman. As long as he took the job, it didn't matter. "I'm grateful." And jealous. But what they'd had or what he'd thought they had was a long time ago.

———

ALL SHE HAD LEFT WAS a horse blanket that was more rag than blanket and a shotgun she'd hidden up in the rafters. They'd even taken her ancient cow Bennie. Who would do such a thing? She didn't want to blame Teagan, but who else?

She ached. She hardly slept. There was no door to keep her safe, and the floor was hard. Her clothes were gone. It made no sense. If it had been an eviction, they would have thrown her stuff out the door. She was hungry and after drinking water from the well, she started in the direction of the garden and root cellar. She didn't get more than a few feet when the sounds of horse's hooves made her cringe, and she ducked behind a tree and waited.

When she recognized the rider, suspicion crowded into her mind. What was Quinn doing here? He appeared surprised when he stared at her house. That made sense, though, for Quinn was too nice to steal a thing. She walked out from behind the tree, but he'd gone inside.

Slowly she walked to the house. "Quinn?"

He walked back through the door, his face full of thunder. "What happened? I heard it was run down but there's nothing here."

Her eyes smarted. "I know. I came home yesterday after talking with Teagan and everything was gone. I don't even have a change of clothes." She sighed and closed her eyes, trying not to cry.

"You stayed here all alone?"

"I had nowhere to go, Quinn. I'm not well received in town anymore. Plus, after walking to your place and back my feet were hurting."

"Here, come sit on the porch with me."

She sat right next to him. It was always easy to be around Quinn.

He took hold of her foot and yanked her shoe off.

"Wait! Oh, that hurts!"

"Because your shoe was stuck to your foot with dried blood." He yanked the other one off and threw it.

"That's all I have! Quinn, why?"

He stood and scooped her up then carried her over and

set her on his horse. Then he pulled himself up behind her. "Because you're not living like this. You've been like a sister to us, and it's shameful we never checked on you. That's why." He spurred his horse and they rode back to the Kavanagh place.

To her mortification, they'd no sooner pulled up in front of the house when Teagan walked out the door. His gaze fell to her feet, and his jaw hardened. "Dolly!" he called. Then he turned back to Gemma. "What happened to your feet?"

Quinn hopped off his horse, turned and lifted her, and then placed her into Teagan's arms.

Her breath stalled in her throat and she ceased all struggles. She was upset and in pain, but she was in his arms again. Their gazes met for a moment, and then they both glanced away. She swallowed hard and tried to be as stiff as possible.

"Relax," he whispered.

"I don't know how to act around you anymore."

"You don't like me. Just act that way but relax." He carried her inside to a little sitting room, where Dolly had gotten a basin of water ready. With gentleness she never would have expected, he sat her on a worn leather couch.

"How did your feet get to be so bad?" Teagan asked.

"I need new shoes." A sharp gasp slid out as Dolly did something that sent spikes of pain across her right foot. "Ouch!"

"I know it hurts, but I have to clean all the broken blisters," Dolly gently told her.

"We have other news, Teagan. Someone took all her things. Completely emptied the house, I don't think the curtains were still there." Quinn shook his head.

"When did this happen?"

Gemma turned her head. "When I got home yesterday, the door was completely off the hinges and on the porch. My hidden rifle was still there, but they took everything else. My clothes, the quilts my mama made, furniture Pa carved, and even the family Bible. I went into the barn and it was empty. My cow… the chickens, all I found was a horse blanket."

"Why didn't you come get one of us?" Teagan sounded frustrated with her.

Gemma sighed and glanced away. "My feet hurt. I slept on the floor with the blanket and the rifle. I wasn't sure what to think."

He leveled a knowing stare on her. "You thought I was involved."

He sure knew how to make her mad. "It crossed my mind for a moment, but I dismissed it. There have been times we've wished ill will toward each other, but you wouldn't leave me with nowhere to go. If I could just borrow a few things, I'll be on my way."

"Honey, you aren't going to go anywhere," Dolly said. "At least not without a pair of shoes. Something is going on, and you can't stay there alone. You'll stay with us, right Teagan?"

Teagan tried to smile and produced a grimace, and Gemma wanted to laugh. He wasn't an actor, that was for sure. He hated the idea of her being here, and she didn't blame him.

"Of course," he said, his voice strained. "And Dolly will make sure you have everything you need. I'm trying to puzzle this all out. You never signed anything over to your husband, did you?"

"Of course not, but once a woman marries, her property becomes her husband's…" She fought back a sob but lost, and it came out sounding like a hiccup. "Oh no, how could he?"

"You think he did this?" Quinn asked, staring at her with his jaw dropped.

"Yes… no. I don't rightly know," she said, hating that she had to keep explaining things. "He already had a wife I didn't know about, but he stole all my money and now it looks like he's sold my land somehow." The heat of anger rushed to her face. "I bet that sneaky banker Victor Lyons is involved." She blinked, abruptly realizing Quinn didn't seem surprised. "You already knew, didn't you? About my husband?"

"That he had a wife and married you anyway?" Quinn asked. He drew a deep breath then nodded. "Teagan told me."

Her face felt as though it was on fire. She nodded and kept her gaze on her fisted hands.

"I explained a few things," Teagan said in a quiet voice.

"It's — I'm grateful. Please tell the rest of your brothers. I don't want to talk about it unless I have to."

"So, it's settled. You'll stay here," Teagan said, obviously taking over. "I can have someone watch your house in case they come back. Mr. Lyons can't resell property that I hold the note on. He'd have to give me the money owed on the loan. I'll ride there tomorrow morning and confront him."

"Th-thank you, Teagan." She couldn't look at him or anyone. She must be cursed. How much bad luck could one person have?

"We'll get new clothes and things for you. I can't imagine having everything just disappear like that."

"Could I borrow your Bible?" She raised her head and met his gaze. He looked so different as though he cared, and she quickly wiped every tear that fell.

SUPPER WAS QUIETER THAN USUAL. Teagan's brothers didn't seem to know what to say for once. Usually they all had an opinion. He looked at them; Quinn, Brogan, Sullivan, Donnell, Murphy, Fitzpatrick, Angus, Rafferty, and Shea. His father had always been extra proud of all the sons he'd fathered, while his mother had kept hoping for a daughter.

"I'm glad you're here with us, Gemma," Sullivan said. "I feel embarrassed that I never thought to check on you when I got back from the war. It's a sad thing when neighbors don't check on one another. It took a lot to get this place back up and running. It looked like a cannon ball went through the house. They must have fought on our land. We find bullets, buttons from uniforms… bones all the time. Oh, I'm sorry. I probably shouldn't have brought up the bones while we're eating."

Gemma nodded. "You're right about the fighting. I hid in the new root cellar I dug, and the ground shook."

"Could you hear people in your house?" Sullivan leaned forward.

"Soldiers took all my food. I dug a new cellar in the woods about a half hour's walk from my house. Shorter if bullets were flying. I stayed there for a few days. No one came near me, which was a relief since I'd also planted a second garden there."

"The last few years haven't been easy," Quinn commented.

"That's for sure," Sullivan agreed.

Teagan felt awful. He should have sent someone to check on Gemma and her family. He'd thought enough about what she'd done to him.

"She's here now, and we'll take good care of her. We must keep watch on her at least until we know who we're dealing with," Teagan told them.

She gave him a small smile. He remembered when her smile would light up a whole room… and his heart. It seems so long ago yet the hurt still felt fresh.

"I'll have the boys haul warm water to your room for a bath," Dolly said. "I put soap and a towel on a stool near the tub. I lent you one of my night gowns and a robe. They'll be long on you, so be careful. And no comments about how I wear old fashioned grandmother bed clothes."

"Now I want to see," Quinn said with a laugh.

Everyone stopped and stared. Quinn never laughed anymore.

"The whole purpose is that the wearer is so covered there is nothing to see. I've seen different versions with buttons and ankle lengths. Some have ribbon on them. I just wear what my mother used to make for me." She huffed. "Why I'm discussing such things with you men, I have no idea. I'll start on the dishes while you boys haul the water."

Teagan smiled and was silent until they were alone. "For a moment I thought she was going to say that there was a lock on the sleeping garment."

"I guess I wear grandma clothes to bed too." Her smile faded. "I suppose the bath was the reason my feet weren't wrapped. A bath will be a real treat compared to the stream."

"Everyone is right, you know," he said sounding contrite. "I should have checked on you. I just didn't know... I figured you wouldn't want to see me. You made it clear you hated me."

Tears filled her eyes. "That was my intent. You had a shotgun trained on your head that day. I needed to be sure you never came back. I never got over the things I said to you, just like I never—" She broke off and took a deep breath. "I knew if I told you why, you'd confront my father, and it wouldn't end well. I couldn't lose either of you. I am sorry, though. I could see the pain in your eyes, and I wanted to die."

He reached over and covered her hand with his. She suddenly stood. "It looks like the water is all in the tub." She practically ran from the room, leaving Teagan stunned.

Her father would have killed him? Her father had always been very kind. They'd had many chats over the years. Something else must have happened, or she was just plain wrong. She hadn't seemed to fake the hate she felt for him when she told him to go away and never come back. Was she lying about what happened, so he'd stop hating her now? He didn't hate her he just didn't want to give his heart to a woman again. It would soothe his soul to believe her, but he couldn't. It made no sense. Something strange was going on, and he'd best keep up his guard.

She could stay until things were cleared up with her land, but she'd have to leave as soon as possible. She'd haunted him for a long time, and he wondered what he had done to make her hate him so. It had gnawed at him until he just couldn't take it anymore. But it had done something to him. He wasn't comfortable around women anymore. He'd lost his confidence with them. Some found it romantic that he brooded. If they only knew the real Teagan. He'd been told he didn't even know how to treat a woman... or what love was.

CHAPTER THREE

$\mathcal{H}$e walked his horse the rest of the way through the back part of the Maguire property to avoid being seen. Their cattle were still mixed in with his. He'd have to get one of the boys to cut them from the herd but for now, the broken fence served his purpose.

He stopped every few minutes and listened. The closer he got, the more convinced he was that someone else was in the woods. He went past the house and hid behind a big oak tree that had been good for kissing behind. It was useful to him now since it was big enough to hide both him and Sandy.

He saw movement in the woods and watched as a man led his horse out. He put his horse into the barn and then headed toward the house. He kicked the fallen door and laughed. Could he be the so-called husband? It made him madder to think of those hands being on Gemma. If he was an impulsive man, he'd be in there right now punching him in the jaw. But he'd wait.

He sat down and made himself comfortable leaning against the trunk. It'd probably be awhile before the man showed his hand. A twig snapped and he sat up, listening.

More twigs snapped, and the shuffling of footsteps on soft ground followed by the rustle of leaves. Someone not well versed in being quiet was coming through the woods from the same direction he'd traveled from.

Leaving Sandy behind, Teagan circled back. Gemma? What was she doing here and leading one of his best horses? He frowned and silently snuck up behind her and wrapped one hand around her waist and the other over her mouth. She struggled then she bit him.

He quickly turned her around and glared at her. Then he put his finger to his lips to indicate silence. He sighed in relief at her nod.

He took the horse and he led her slowly toward the tree, hoping that the person in the house hadn't heard them. He tied the other horse next to his dun and took Gemma's hand. Then he pulled her down to the ground by the tree trunk.

"What are you doing here?" he whispered.

"I'm trying to find out what's going on," she hissed back.

"I thought Quinn was watching you."

"I told him I'd be back. I just didn't say when." She flashed him a smile.

He glared back.

The man came out of the house, disappointment etched into his features.

Gemma gasped and then put her hand over her mouth.

Judging from her reaction, this was the man who had falsely married her. As much as he wanted to confront the man, Teagan decided to wait. He doubted Richard Parks would tell them anything unless he had to. He studied Parks. He certainly wasn't anything to look at. Skinny like a starving coyote that couldn't figure out how to get in the henhouse, he had stringy hair that fell across his face and hung over his shoulders. It might have been any color under all that dirt.

Richard stalked to the barn and rode out on his horse. This time he didn't go through the woods; he rode down the dirt road.

Teagan tilted his head and regarded Gemma, disbelief rifling through his system. "You married *him*? I expected someone suave and handsome."

"Oh, please. Like I had so many choices. Besides he was handsome when I met him." She gestured toward the house. "He was looking for something, but what? Something he left behind? Something of my father's? I had nothing hidden. Why not just wait until I was away from the house and search it like a normal thief would have?"

"That part, I believe, has something to do with the banker. Shall we go inside while it's still bright and see what we can find?"

She smiled. "I think we shall."

He stared at her feet. They were wrapped heavily in bandages. They had to be paining her. Why couldn't she just have stayed at his house and rested?

He didn't offer her his arm. The less they touched the better.

As soon as they were inside, she turned in a wide circle then stopped. "I don't know where to begin. It's plain to see the place is empty."

"Loose floorboards, loose rocks around the fireplace. Behind a wall..." He surveyed the tiny room. "Well, yours are all single walled, so we'll start at the fireplace."

She nodded and went to the massive fireplace. She took the right side while he took the left, and they both started pushing and shaking the rocks. He was about halfway up from the floor when she released a tiny cry.

"I found a loose one!"

He shifted to join her, and they both pulled and wiggled.

The stone was in there good, but it was definitely loose. Finally, it gave way and tumbled to the hearth with a thud.

In the small space behind it, was stuffed a gold ring and a small bit of money. "Well, we found something," he admitted. "Just not what I think Richard is looking for."

"No, I suppose not." She stared at the ring for a moment. "This is my daddy's wedding ring. He must've left this for Mama to sell if she needed to." She tucked the money and ring into her skirt pocket. They continued pushing and pulling on the rounded stones but came up empty.

After a while, they started on the floorboards.

Teagan stomped his foot in the middle of the room, eliciting a hollow sound. "You have a lot of loose floorboards."

"I don't have any nails to fix them. That's why the roof leaks too." She turned away but not before he saw her face turn crimson.

He'd embarrassed her, and he hadn't meant to. There wasn't anything in the main rooms. They stepped into her parent's room and the pried floorboards were thrown around the room. Gemma shook her head and then got on her hands and knees looking in all the holes.

Teagan checked the rest of the floor but found nothing. After giving it some thought, they went to her room, but the floor appeared untouched. None of the floorboards showed signs of being loose. With a little effort, he pried up a couple but didn't find a thing.

"Maybe we're not on the right track," he mused aloud. "But he looked confident when he went in. Like he knew what he was looking for and where to find it. I wonder if anyone was around here last night… It might be too late, but I'll have the place guarded and the fence fixed so your cattle stay on my property."

"Just how many head are they?"

"I'd say at least thirty. More than enough to pay any loans.

I think someone was counting on us not talking. But the Kavanaghs work for what they have. We don't take cattle from others."

They walked to the horses, and he helped her onto the saddle before he mounted his. There was a lot to think about. Too bad he hadn't a clue where to begin.

He glanced at Gemma, taking in her confident seat in the saddle, the loose hold she had on the reins. She sure was pretty. "I'd forgotten how good of a rider you are."

She stiffened but otherwise acted as though she didn't hear him. "You mentioned you had a Bible I could use?"

"I'll get it for you when we get home. I think it a good idea if we attend church together. I want people to know you're under the Kavanagh's protection. Maybe it'll cut down on the traffic at your place."

"What is that supposed to mean, Teagan Kavanagh? If you're implying, I entertain men, you can just forget it. I will never as long as I live."

The vehemence in her voice gave him pause, but he had to ask. "What about the big family you wanted to have?"

"Teagan, there is only one way that I know of to make a child, and I refuse to allow myself to be touched like that ever again. Once I'm settled enough and I make the house look nice, I plan to see about adopting a child."

"You have to be married." He bit his tongue, wishing he'd held the words inside. The hurt and worry on her face was a bit much to take. "I'm sure there are exceptions," he hastened to add.

Her face didn't brighten any. If anything, she looked to have lost her best friend.

Was he purposely trying to hurt her? A slap across the face would have been easier. It was obvious Teagan didn't believe her about her father having him killed if she said yes to his marriage proposal. It sounded farfetched, even to her, and she had lived it. Her father had always acted as though he liked Teagan, and then suddenly the Kavanaghs were the enemy. Were the Kavanaghs even aware of her father's hatred?

It didn't seem they were. Seeing Richard unnerved her. At the time she had refused him, she'd never thought to see him again and that had been just fine with her. She blamed herself for the position she was in now. She still had to go to town to buy new clothes. It had been a while since she'd purchased anything for herself besides essential things like flour.

"Am I to talk to Mr. Lyons in town today or just go to the store?"

"Neither. Have no doubt you're in danger. I'll have Dolly buy a few things, and you can sew a few dresses. You do sew, don't you?"

Why didn't he just knock her off her horse? Her heart ached more every time he opened his mouth. She'd made him a beautiful shirt out of fine material, but clearly, he didn't remember. He acted as though he liked it at the time. She just rode right by him. He didn't deserve an answer.

She rode to the barn, and Shea stepped out of the shadows. Without being asked, he lifted her down. "Here you go. I'll take care of Thomas for you."

She blinked in surprise. "The horse is named Thomas?"

"Yes, it is, and you're lucky you still have your hide. Teagan never allows us to ride him."

She thanked him and went to the house, purposely ignoring Teagan as he rode in. If he planned to break another piece of her heart, he was too late. There hadn't been anything to break in a long time.

"There you are!" Dolly said. "Ready to go to town, or do you want to freshen up?"

"She's not going," Teagan answered for her.

"I'll be in danger," Gemma replied, trying to keep the peace. "If I give you a small list, could you pick me up a few things?"

"Put new shoes and some boots on the list, Dolly."

Gemma ignored him and sat down at the table waiting for him to go away. He wasn't cooperating. "Dolly, I don't need much. I can sew anything I need so whatever you find that isn't expensive… umm, except for anything brown will be fine." She looked down at her faded brown dress. "All I've worn for years is brown. I can make my underthings. I think if you get anything readymade someone is bound to notice that it's not your size."

Teagan gave a nod. "Get her a few readymade things in your size, Dolly. She can alter them for now."

"I can probably go down a couple sizes and no one would even notice. I'll just play it by ear."

"Thank you, Dolly, I appreciate it," Gemma said. Getting away from Teagan was first on her list. It was too hard to pretend nothing had happened. It was too hard knowing he didn't like her… well, probably hated her.

She went into her room and closed the door. The day was full of sunshine but not for her. Somehow it was lonelier than being at her ranch alone. At the ranch she didn't have any expectations, and she didn't dare to hope for any change. Just how did someone stop hoping? If she knew, her life would have been free from so much hurt.

Being here enhanced the fact that she really didn't have anyone. She was on her own and she never thought she would be. Sometime after her mother died and her father didn't come back from the war, a piece of her died. She did her best to keep the ranch going, but things turned dire, and that was the only reason she had married Richard. It would have been nice if someone had told her about his gambling. Or his wife. She'd had an idea that he was stepping out on her since he stayed away all night.

To think she had grown up in this town, went to school with most of the people, and no one came to see if she was doing well after Richard took off. She'd gone over and over it in her mind. What had she done? Had she been rude to someone? Had she insulted someone? Was she just unlikable? Finally, she had reached the conclusion that she must be the type of person people didn't like. She had read her Bible every day, looking for clues on how to make people think her likeable. She volunteered to be on committees in the community, but they always just said they'd let her know and never got back to her. The last one had been for a town dance. She'd offered to pour the punch and clean up after, but they told her the wrong date and excluded her.

She'd never been outgoing. She had always been more on the quiet side. It had been hard to go into town and seek to volunteer. To have the dance and not tell her was extremely insulting, but she had finally gotten the message. They didn't want her around.

It seemed her heart had been hurt more in the last several years than it ever had before, and being an adult wasn't always easy. Ranch work usually kept her too busy to contemplate the why of it all day. Though she prayed on it each night.

Teagan didn't want her here, but right now she didn't have a choice. She waited until she heard the doors shut and quietly left her room. She borrowed a straw hat hanging on a peg and grabbed a basket. The Kavanagh's garden wasn't far from their house.

She kneeled on the soil and weeded the whole garden, crawling along the rows a little at a time. Then she picked only what needed picking. Next, she hauled water from the well and watered the plants. It was a garden big enough to feed everyone including the hands.

She stood and lifted the basket. It was nice and full. She'd start a stew while Dolly was shopping. There was enough time to make it for supper. She reached the kitchen, and the mess astounded her. Ten men, no make that nine, since Quinn had driven Dolly to town, had made this mess. Just who did they think would clean it all up?

They had gone through all the bread and ham. Sighing, she put her basket down and rolled up her sleeves. They had a hand pump sink, which made things much easier, but they could have at least cleared the table. It took over one-half hour before it looked presentable. She cut the beef into cubes and browned those in an iron pot. Next, she added flour and stirred in some water. Then she washed the vegetables and set to chopping them. Lastly, she added all the vegetables.

The sound of the wagon made her smile. She was excited at the prospect of sewing a new dress. She went outside and saw Teagan helping Dolly down. Dolly glanced over and bestowed a wide smile on Gemma.

"Wait until you see the yard goods. I haven't seen such a selection in a long time. It was sheer joy picking colors and such." She reached into the back of the wagon and grabbed a crate.

Teagan took it from her and followed them both inside.

Dolly acted as though it was Christmas. Her eyes glowed with each new thing she took out of the crate and handed to Gemma. The cotton material was in shades of green, blue, yellow, pink, all in calico and gingham patterns. There were ribbons and lace and pretty buttons.

"This must have cost a fortune, Dolly. I didn't need all this."

"Quinn told me to get them." Dolly's smile widened. "He added the ribbons."

Gemma's face heated. "It's all so beautiful."

There was very soft white material for underthings, and then there was softer and sheerer white cloth. She looked at Dolly and tilted her head.

"That's for nightgowns. I've never felt anything so delicate."

"Quinn?"

Dolly nodded.

"Thank you, I know how expensive all this is, and I promise to pay you back somehow."

Dolly chuckled. "I'd say you already did. I saw the garden as we drove by. You must have spent hours in it." She sniffed. "And I do believe I smell stew cooking!"

Quinn brought in a few more crates and there was a comb, brush, and mirror, all set in silver. She sat and stared, overwhelmed.

Teagan cleared his throat. "I remembered you once had such a set. And there are shoes in here somewhere." He gestured to the mound of packages. "I need to do some paperwork." As he talked, he glanced at her. "See you at supper."

She watched him go. "Thank you, Dolly and Quinn, for getting all this. It'll keep me busy."

Quinn tipped his hat and went back outside.

Dolly went to one last crate and pulled out two pretty dresses. One was a dusty rose color and the other was an emerald green. "These are the readymade dresses. I thought I could help you at least take them up later this evening."

"You thought of everything. My heart was so sore and

heavy today, but between you and God, I feel much better." Gemma sat down. "Dolly can I ask you something?"

"You sure can."

"Why don't people like me? I've known most of the people in town for a long time, yet I feel excluded. No, I *know* I'm being excluded. I don't understand what I've done. They don't want my help at gatherings. I missed the last dance because they told me the wrong date. We used to all be friends. I don't know, it just hurts is all."

"I don't think it's as much you as it is them. Some folks have the notion you knew about Richard Parks being married but lived as his wife anyway. The worst part is, something like that can't really be defended. Either they believe you or they don't. I know the hurt just makes you feel alone. All you can do is pray that the hurt goes away for yourself. The others won't change. But you can pray for comfort and peace."

"You're right." She sighed. "Teagan was going to loan me a Bible."

Dolly went into the other room and brought back a big leather-bound book. "This is the only one I can think of. It's the family Bible. Just don't throw it at anyone."

"I promise I won't." She put the heavy book on her bed and then went back and put the supplies away.

CHAPTER FOUR

The horses were beautiful. Many looked like thoroughbreds. Which brother had decided to breed horses? Gemma put her hand out to touch the nose of a beautiful bay.

"Don't touch my horses."

She turned and there stood Brogan looking angrier than she'd ever seen him. "They are great horses, Brogan."

"You might have flattered your way into Teagan's good graces, but I have a very long memory. I remember just how broken Teagan was after you were done with him. Why did you lead him on? Was it fun to have a man fall in love with you? Did it feel powerful to turn him away? Did you laugh about it later?" He snorted. "I bet it was good for your ego."

"No, it—"

"I don't want to hear your lies. Did you know Teagan joined up the next day and Quinn went with him? Teagan was reckless, not caring if he returned home or not, and while he never got a scratch on him, Quinn did. I blame you for it all. When I saw you sitting at our table, I wanted to jump over it, grab you and throw you out the door. Now

33

you're staying here. Have you thought for one single second what your presence here is doing to Teagan?"

Why wasn't she close to the door so she could just run out? She deserved some of his disdain, it was true, but he didn't know the whole story. He was only looking out for his brother. Side stepping, she hoped to get by him, but he blocked her way.

"I want you out of here tonight. I don't care what excuse you give to Teagan, but your invitation to stay here has been revoked. Understand?" he practically growled at her.

She shook her head and tried to get around him again. He grabbed her arm.

"I asked if you understood."

"Yes, yes I understand. Just let me go." As soon as he released her, she ran out of the barn. She hadn't known any of what Brogan had just told her. But he was right. It *was* her fault. Somehow, she had to make things right. Starting with finding employment so she could take care of herself.

She looked down at her new dress and new boots. She was presentable now. Maybe she could find a position in town. Turning south, she walked toward the town. Going back home was what she really wanted to do, but she was too scared, and it would be a hardship to live with no furniture or even a decent blanket.

It was a long, dry dusty walk, and she dreaded every step. It would be all right, she tried to convince herself. Maybe it had been a big misunderstanding about the dance. Certainly, people wouldn't be so cruel to exclude her like she thought they had. The town seemed to grow every day. There was now a barber shop and a new doctor. Hopefully Mrs. Miller still ran her boarding house. But before she could think of a place to stay, she'd need a job first.

She started at one end of the street at the Yellow Rose Café and worked her way through every establishment, but the answer was always the same: no one was hiring. She crossed the street, hurried passed Bobbie's Saloon, and knocked on the doctor's door.

A man about thirty years old with the blondest hair she had ever seen opened the door. "May I help you? I'm Doctor Bright."

"It's very nice to meet you, Dr. Bright. My name is Gemma Maguire, and I'm looking for a job."

"Well come on in." He stepped aside.

She entered and stepped around a stack of crates. There were boxes everywhere. "You haven't had time to set up."

"No, but I could use some help. I'm staying at Mrs. Miller's while I get organized." He gestured at the chaotic office. "I have a feeling it'll be awhile before I get the living quarters set up."

"That's why I need a job, so I can afford to stay at the boarding house too."

"When would you like to start?"

"I need to pack my things, but I could be here in the morning if that's fine?" She held her breath waiting for his answer.

A smile broke out across his face. "Well, I'll see you in the morning then."

She returned his smile. "I'll be here. Thank you so much!" Nearly giddy with the first excitement she had felt in ages, she opened the door and let herself out.

Next, she stopped at the boarding house to see if there was a room for her.

"Well… I don't know…" Mrs. Miller seemed hesitant. "Most of my boarders are gentlemen…"

"Please," said Gemma. "I will be working for Dr. Bright, and I need a place to live."

"Oh, well, in that case…" Mrs. Miller's face brightened,

and she became more enthusiastic. "I could reduce the rent if you'd help with the cleaning after supper."

"That would be wonderful. I'll see you tomorrow."

Happy but tired, she set out for the Kavanagh ranch. She bet there'd be many happy men when she told them of her plans. Her feet were killing her before she was halfway back, but she didn't have a choice; she had to finish the walk, so she kept going. Tears of both pain and joy stung her eyes when finally, she was there. She opened the door, walked to the sofa, and sat down. Her feet stung, and she was afraid if she took her shoes off, she'd never get them back on when her feet swelled.

She needed water, but she'd wait until she caught her breath. A sense of not being alone stole over her. She felt his gaze on her before she turned her head. Teagan was home.

"Where have you been?"

She knew that barely calm voice. It was the one he used when he really wanted to yell.

She sat up straighter and pushed out her chin. "I found a job and a place to live. I start tomorrow."

"Why?"

The question deflated a bit of her bravado. "Teagan… I'm not wanted here. I'm not your problem, and after what happened between us, I highly doubt you really want me here. Brogan told me everything about how you joined up and were reckless and Quinn getting hurt. It's my fault, and I can't stay here knowing that." She heaved a sigh. "If only I'd been braver and disobeyed my father, but if I had, you might be dead. So, I'm not sure that would have been the answer." She stood. "I need to get some water and then pack. I do appreciate all you've done for me."

"What are you talking about?" He finally seemed to find his voice. "Are you insane? You can't be traipsing all over with Richard out there. How I feel makes no difference. And Brogan doesn't speak for me. Your safety comes first!"

"No, it doesn't," she told him as a wave of sadness struck. "You come first, and me being here isn't good for you!"

"Now I know you've been dropped on your head!"

"You are infur—" She could barely gasp as his lips covered hers.

The kiss felt angry at first, but it gentled, and his lips felt so right, so unbearably right. He lifted his head and looked into her eyes. She dropped her gaze and stared at a button on his shirt. The pain was raw, and her eyes smarted. This was the way they should have been, but it was too late now.

Stifling a cry, Gemma pulled away and ran to her room. She closed the door and leaned against it, her heart pounding hard against her chest. Now what?

SHE PUT the last of her things in the back of the wagon. Teagan had left the house, slamming the door behind him when she told everyone she was leaving. The rest of breakfast had been silent. Quinn was going to drive her. The others didn't seem to care much except for Brogan who wore a look of victory.

It was for the best. She couldn't look at Teagan without thinking *what if?* She couldn't tell him the reason her father wanted him dead either. It wasn't just Teagan; he wanted all Kavanaghs dead. When her mother finally talked about it before she died, she said her heart was ground to dust and she always felt that she never gave Gemma any love, since she didn't have any left to give. It was hard to hear, and it'd been hard to bear. Her mother hadn't been affectionate, and it had hurt.

"Ready?" Quinn asked.

"Yes, let me just grab my wrap and thank Dolly."

The older woman smiled. "I have a feeling you'll be back. You take care of yourself and remember you have friends here."

"I know." Gemma went out the door and quietly closed it behind her. She had no plans to ever come back.

Quinn wasn't one for conversation, so the silence didn't bother her. He stopped the wagon in front of Mrs. Miller's then jumped to the ground and helped Gemma down. As she turned to survey her surroundings, a familiar figure hustled across the street and smiled at her.

"I'm glad you're here."

"Dr. Bright, this is my neighbor, Quinn Kavanagh."

"Call me Joshua. It's nice to meet you, Quinn." They shook hands, and she could tell by the look in his eyes that Quinn was sizing up the doctor.

"Treat her right," Quinn said softly. "And if there is any trouble or that man Richard comes for her, come get us. She shouldn't be living in town, but if you will protect her, then I guess it's fine."

"What man?" Mrs. Miller demanded in a harsh tone as she walked down her front steps with her eyes narrowed.

"The man who married her but was already married," Quinn explained. "The one who left with all her money. He was spotted yesterday."

Gemma never wanted to kick anyone as hard as she did Quinn. She could tell by Mrs. Miller's frown she'd lost her place to live, and now Joshua also looked indecisive.

"Protect her? I don't have a firearm," Joshua said.

Quinn smiled and turned his triumphant gaze on Gemma. Anger welled as the truth dawned on her. He'd done the whole thing on purpose. And didn't he look quite pleased with himself, standing there with a wide grin on his face.

Both the doctor and Mrs. Miller talked at the same time. "I don't think—"

Gemma held her hand up. "I understand. No hard feelings." She walked to the wagon and climbed up. Flames of embarrassment licked at her face. She stared at her hands, too humiliated to have anyone see her discomfort.

Quinn whistled a happy tune as he drove them right out of town. She stole a glance at him and seethed. He was still happy with himself. Even if some people didn't know that Richard had already been married, they all would now. She'd find no work in town—or friends. She would bet the whole debacle with Quinn messing up her plan was Teagan's idea. If he was trying to get back at her, he'd done a good job.

She stared out at the scenery as the wagon brought them closer and closer to the Kavanaghs. She didn't know what else to do. She'd dug so many holes in her yard looking for her father's buried money, but she hadn't found any in a long time.

Well, she still had her cellar and garden, so she wouldn't starve. Tomorrow she was going home.

Once they were in front of the house, she jumped down without waiting for help and went around the woods on the side of the house. Being alone was what she craved. She followed a dirt path until she came to the big rock next to the stream and sat on it. Why? Why had they done it? Revenge? It was a good enough reason, she supposed. Teagan had probably laughed the whole time she was loading the wagon and then waited with glee for her plans to be destroyed. It wasn't fair. She had never asked for his help.

Seeing him was too hard. Being around him was near impossible. If things had been different, they would have had children by now... Or perhaps not. She hadn't enjoyed being a wife, and she never wanted to be touched again. She kicked at the dirt as she realized she had nothing, not even a pot to cook with, at her place. Could it have been Teagan who'd cleared out her house so she couldn't live there? She'd dismissed the possibility earlier, but it made more sense than anything else she'd come up with. She'd stay out of his way. The war had left many places empty. She could scavenge the things she needed. But no... She shook her head. It had been too long; there'd be nothing left to scavenge.

She had one choice. The same choice she'd had before; she needed to get married. Finding a widower with children would be the best option. She knew a few, Dolly probably knew others. and if she didn't give away her intent, the Kavanaghs might know a few. She'd play Teagan's game but just until she found a man who would only want a mother for his children.

They were probably wondering where she was; she needed to get back. Teagan might think he'd won, and that wouldn't do.

———

AFTER WALKING INTO THE HOUSE, she helped herself to a glass of water and then sat down in the front room. Quinn must have taken care of the horses and the wagon, and by now, her belongings were probably back in the bedroom she had used. She had plenty of sewing she could do. She drank her water and brought the glass into the kitchen. Looking out the window, she noted everyone seemed to be busy. They sure had many people working for them as well as themselves. They must be doing well. It was nice they had rebuilt; few folks were able to pick up where they had left off.

She'd tried her best but to no avail. Oh well, it was all in the past. A sigh slipped out. If only that were true. Richard was out there. What was his plan and why? Maybe if she looked around a bit more, she'd find whatever Richard was after. And that banker—he was in on it too. It must be something Richard had found out about after he had left, but she didn't have a notion what it might be.

Movement caught her eye. Teagan was headed to the house. She quickly walked away from the window and headed into her room. She'd get her sewing. There was no way she'd allow him to think he'd won. It would be over her dead body before he knew how miserable he'd made her.

CHAPTER FIVE

*I*t had been two weeks since her humiliating ride into town. Gemma had spent that time sewing and gathering information. She found out about four possible widowers she might approach. There was Ed Calver and his three boys ages eight months, two years, and five years old. He was a farmer and raised pigs. His house was said to be sound.

There was also John Dew, who she had met before. He was nice enough, but he never smiled. He had five children; ages three years old up to seven years old. Three boys and two girls. He raised cattle on his "patch of dirt". Shea wasn't impressed with the man at all. Supposedly he made no repairs and the children ran around in rags.

Adam Johnson had a nice house and a promising ranch. He had four children ranging in age from a one-year-old to seven years old. The oldest was a girl. He had supposedly sworn he'd never marry again.

Last was Cal Meagher and his brood of six children. The ages went from three months to six years old and there were twins in there somewhere, all boys. It was said he was desperate. His ranch was nice, and he had a housekeeper, but he wanted a mother for the children.

She'd never been around children, so Cal and his six boys seemed a bit daunting. Luckily there was a barn raising at his ranch the next day and Gemma had been busy making pies and putting the last touches on her new yellow calico dress. She'd sewn a bonnet to match and for a change she was excited about something. She would try to get to know each man. She didn't want to be choosey, but she had to be sure she'd find a man who would never touch her. How was she to approach that subject?

She'd prayed while she was sewing, and she felt good about herself. She hadn't knowingly sinned with Richard. There was bound to be talk, but she'd have to stay strong and ignore it. Plus, she'd be with the Kavanaghs. That alone would dissuade most from making remarks.

She hummed as she stepped into the kitchen to put the pies in the pie safe. But she stopped short with a gasp at the sight that awaited her. One piece had been taken out of each of the six pies. She shook her head. What had happened? There was only one dirty plate and fork... And all her hard work for naught. She wanted to cry but that feeling quickly passed as anger rose. Who would do such a thing? Of course, she had a ranch full of suspects.

Did they *want* to keep her at home? Well, that would not work. She was still attending, pies or no pies. She went to the window and tried to see who was around, but she didn't see anyone, which was strange. There was always someone around. She turned, grabbed her pies, and one by one put them gently into the pie safe. She wouldn't waste them just because someone had ruined them. Disgusted, she shook her head and left the kitchen.

There had been tension in the house between her and Teagan and a few of the brothers didn't seem thrilled she was there. But Brogan was the only one who had been vocal about it, and he didn't care who was around when he opened his mouth.

There was also tension between Teagan and Brogan. She needed to leave before she destroyed their family. Her house had been watched for the last week and a half, but Teagan had finally put an end to that. Now he had men fixing the place up and shoring up the barn during the day. Maybe he could get more money for doing those things when he sold the land.

There had been some happy years for her there, but the happiness had gone away when she had been forced to refuse Teagan's marriage proposal. All she had ever wanted was to be happy, but it didn't happen for her. Gemma wandered upstairs and into her room. It was a bright and cheerful room. It was a lighter green color, the color of a fern. She picked up her yellow dress, wanting to be sure there wasn't a single wrinkle in it. But the dress fell apart in her hands, and she couldn't contain her outcry.

It had been ripped apart and there would be no repairing it. Even the bonnet had a nasty tear in it. Her hands shook as she examined each piece. Taking a deep breath, she walked down the stairs and out the back door. She didn't stop until she got to the creek, and then the tears poured down her face. Someone really hated her and wanted her gone.

Teagan hadn't done it. He wasn't mean like that. When he was mad, he made it known outright. She had to leave. No way could she live with such hatred. Her house was probably done enough that she could live there. She turned toward the Kavanagh house but couldn't bring herself to go back. She'd go the longer way to her house by following the creek. Until

Teagan said otherwise, she'd assume it was hers. The door was most certainly fixed by now, and that was all she needed. Her shotgun was still hidden as far as she knew, and she needed to work on her garden.

It was just as well she wasn't going to the barn raising, since the Kavanaghs wouldn't be offering her any protection as she'd once thought. But she sure wished she had someone's shoulder to cry on. Loneliness filled her before she even got halfway to her empty house. Hopefully, the workmen would be gone by the time she got there. And at least her feet didn't hurt as much and they weren't bleeding. It had been foolish to run away with none of her things, but she'd be just fine. She could do this.

After the garden was taken care of and fenced in better, she'd go after her cattle. She could sell some. Then she'd have the money to make payments to Teagan, and perhaps she need not rush into another marriage. Sometimes having a plan made her feel better, but it didn't this time. It didn't really matter what she did. No one cared. If she kept to herself and didn't cause trouble, she'd be forgotten once again.

The house came into view, and she stopped and stared. She'd never seen it look so fine. Not even when her parents had been alive. So much of the wood had been replaced it was almost new. She walked to the front, and a sob bubbled out of her throat. The steps were fixed and whitewashed, and the door was a new one. The windows looked new too. That crazy man... Teagan shouldn't have gone to so much trouble. There was even wood chopped and stacked.

It seemed strange to walk up fixed steps and open the new door. The floor was nailed down, and as she stared at it in wonder, more tears fell. Her horse blanket was still there, folded in the corner. She'd bring it with her to the cellar.

There was no sense staying at the house tonight; they'd just come and get her.

She grabbed her shotgun and blanket and started out for her garden and the root cellar. Perhaps she'd been too proud of her pies and her dress. It wasn't good to be too prideful. Too bad she didn't have a Bible in her cellar. She had food, though, and she had stored water there too. It wasn't the most comfortable place to sleep but it would do and she would be safe.

Usually she enjoyed the pleasant walk, but today her heart had no joy in it. She kept her rifle with her as she weeded her garden. She'd have enough to get her through winter once she picked and put them up, preserved for the cold days. For now, there was enough to pick to fill her growling stomach. She pulled opened the door and climbed down the makeshift steps to the cellar.

She could sense something was wrong.

"WHICH ONE OF you boneheads ate the pie?" Teagan was livid. "Who eats one slice out of each pie? Someone who didn't want Gemma to have anything to bring to the barn raising tomorrow."

"It wasn't me," insisted Shea, "but you should know she's been asking questions about all the men without wives who have children. I think she's look-in' for a husband."

"And that is your business because?" Teagan stared him down.

"Teagan," Quinn piped up. "No one wants to see you hurt. We can see every time you look at her that you love her still."

Sullivan stepped forward. "I ate one piece."

Donnell stepped forward. "I ate one piece."

Murphy nodded. "Me too."

Fitzpatrick smiled. "It was superb."

Angus shook his head. "We were just trying to help you."

"Yea, it was for you, Teagan," Rafferty commented.

"It's still not right. What if I let all the steers you rounded up go? What if I scattered them and a whole day's work was ruined?"

"Not the same thing," Quinn objected.

Teagan narrowed his eyes and shook his head. "Where is she?"

"I saw her go into the house and waited for her to come running out yellin' at us, but she didn't," Shea said.

"Gemma?" Teagan called. He went up the steps and walked into her room. Her dress was in tatters on her bed. What in the world? Picking up a couple of the pieces, he realized her dress had been torn apart. Had she done this? He remembered the glow in her cheeks as she'd sewn the dress. He grabbed up the remnants, carried them down the stairs, and threw them on the dining table.

Shea whistled. "She must have been mad!"

"Did you see anyone else around the house?" Teagan asked.

"No, just us," denied Shea. "She was happy when she sewed. I bet it looked real good on her too."

Teagan glared at the rest of his brothers. "Shea is the only one around here who talks?"

Quinn handed Teagan his hat. "Come on. Let's go find her."

In short order, they saddled their horses and rode to the Maguire house. Teagan sighed in disappointment when they found the place empty. He took his hat off and hit it against his thigh. "Doesn't she know she's in danger? I don't mind helping her—I *want* to help her—but she doesn't seem to want my help."

"I know she was looking forward to the barn raising. But

she *was* asking about all the men who had lost their wives. Why, I don't know. If she wanted to marry, she could have her pick of men."

Teagan shook his head. "Not after what Richard Parks did. Even though Gemma didn't know he was already married, society blames the woman. It doesn't matter that he's a no-good scoundrel. All that matters is Gemma lived as his wife and the marriage wasn't legal. It's not fair to her, it's just the way things are. I don't know when she's telling the truth or lying to me. She said her father had a gun pointed at my head the day I proposed and if she hadn't refused me and made sure I'd never come around again, he planned to pull the trigger. Quinn, our families had been close at one time. I don't understand. I always thought it understood we'd marry. I'd loved her since forever."

"I remember something going on, and it was all hushed up. It had something to do with Brogan, but I can't begin to imagine what. I remember an argument I heard after Ma died and it was heated. I left as soon as I heard Brogan's name. I just didn't want to know. Ma always treated him differently."

"Did she? I never noticed."

Quinn smiled. "Of course not. With you being the oldest you were basking in being the favorite of both Ma and Pa."

"Well the favorite had more chores than anyone else." Teagan released a wry laugh. "I could never get away with anything but the rest of you were just boys being boys. I often wished I was one of the younger ones. I would have liked to have played."

"You know how to play chess." Quinn chuckled.

"I know our ranch is big, but I wouldn't say we were high society or anything, yet father raised me to be or think I was better than others." He grinned. "I can run the ranch and play chess. It doesn't seem to be a very long list of accomplishments."

"Big enough, Teagan, big enough."

"Where do you think she is?"

"I've been thinking on that. Who cut up her dress? I can't imagine she did it, not if she planned to find a husband. Dolly has the day off, so we don't know who was in and out of the house but if a stranger was around, we'd have known about it. She probably has other dresses she can wear. She was sewing a blue one too, I think."

"I think between the pies and the dress, the barn raising is spoiled for her. I wonder when the last time she had a bit of fun was?" Teagan looked at the horizon. "It sounded as though she was on her own for a while dealing with soldiers that came by. I'm thankful she wasn't harmed. I have to say it was right smart to build a new root cellar and grow a garden away from the house."

"Did she mention what direction the garden is?" Quinn cocked his left brow.

Hope blossomed in Teagan's heart. "No, but I bet we can find her tracks. Good thinking, Quinn."

They both got off their horses and searched the ground at the forest edges.

"Over here!" Quinn called.

"We must leave the horses." Teagan said as he took Sandy and led him to a stall in the barn. Quinn did the same.

They followed the tracks, and it wasn't long before they saw the garden. It was rather big and freshly weeded. It took a minute or two to find the door to the root cellar. Tall grass grew all around it hiding it from view. Very clever.

They stood next to the door. "Do we knock?" Quinn asked with a nervous chuckle.

"I suppose so." Teagan flashed him a smile before he bent

over and knocked on the door in the ground. "It's Teagan and Quinn, Gemma."

The door slowly pushed up. She looked as though she'd been crying, and his heart went out to her.

"I'm glad we found you," Quinn told her. "I'll just leave you two to talk. I have a lot of work to do, and I'm behind." Then he walked away before they had a chance to respond.

Her eyes were big, and she looked bewildered.

"This is a great place you have here."

"Don't tease me. I've had enough for one day." She crossed her arms around her waist.

"Can I see?"

"The cellar?"

"Yes, the cellar."

"Follow me. Careful where you step. Someone has been digging in here. Probably Richard. He never came here with me. I didn't even think he knew where to look." She led the way into the damp smelling dugout.

"This is much bigger than I imagined. It must have taken you a long while to dig it."

Shrugging her shoulder, she gave him a hint of a smile. "When it's a life or death situation, you'd be surprised how quickly you can accomplish things."

It was deep enough that he could stand up straight. There was plenty of dug up dirt. He saw her one tattered blanket and a lantern. There was food preserved in jars, staples such as flour and cornmeal stored in barrels. "You spent plenty of nights here." It was a statement not a question.

She nodded. "I can lock it from inside."

"Why didn't you come here when you saw your house was empty?"

"I wanted to catch whoever had done it.

"Makes sense." He inspected her in the lamp light. Her eyes were red and puffy. Her nose was red and there was a look of defeat about her. "I'm sorry about what happened at the house. The boys ate the pie pieces so you wouldn't have pies to give to widowers."

Confusion flashed in her eyes. "That makes no sense."

Teagan shrugged. "Seems they think we're meant to be together. I think they thought they were helping me. I explained it in cattle terms, so they'd understand how much work you did and how they ruined it. I'm sorry."

"I was furious then hurt, but I figured I'd bring pre-cut pies. There will be one less, but I think it would have been fine. Then I went upstairs to make sure my dress was free of wrinkles. Did you see it? The dress?" Tears glistened in her eyes.

Heaving a sigh, Teagan gave a nod. "When I was looking for you, I found the dress. No one admitted to doing it. It would have looked right pretty on you, and I know you put a lot of time into making it."

"And the bonnet," she whispered as she sat down on the bed she'd made down there. "My world is being upended again, and it kills me to admit it, but I don't feel strong enough to fight my way back again. It's been one mistake after another, one bad decision after another, and I'm left with no one I can turn to. You've been very kind to me, and I thank you, but it's not your job to look after me. Teagan, you should be married with children by now. Your life should be rich with the love of a good woman, and I'm surprised you're not courting anyone. You have a good future ahead of you and you need to take a chance on it."

He sat next to her and waited for her to move away, but she didn't. "I'm doing what I want to do. I'm making the ranch one of the best in the state. I have all my brothers and I didn't think we'd all come through the war. I want a wife and children one day, but I don't think I'm ready to look just yet. Why are you looking for a widower to marry?"

Her face flashed over to crimson. "I thought it for the best. Sometimes people in dire need aren't picky. Plus, I figured they already had children and I wouldn't be expected to present them with more."

"Richard hurt you, didn't he?"

She turned her head away and wrung her hands. "It was me. I'm a failure in that aspect. Yes, he hurt me because I wasn't teachable, he said. He didn't hit me, but it hurt too… He stayed out all night and at first, I was relieved. My body needed time to heal. Then I heard about all the women at Bobbie's Saloon, and it hurt in a different way, but I think it hurt my pride, mostly. Everyone knew, of course, and I was the newlywed who couldn't keep her husband happy. At least they probably whispered that behind closed doors. I'm not acceptable anymore, so that is why I thought a widower might just need someone to tend to his children."

Teagan gathered her into his arms and pulled her close until her head lay on his shoulder. She held her body stiff. Her bones were more prominent than they had been before the war, but holding her brought back memories. "What about love?"

"I'll love the children."

"I don't think it's the same thing." He kissed her forehead. "I'm sorry for how things worked out for you."

"Thank you." She released a choked sob. "I thought I had everything I ever wanted. I loved fiercely and was loved in return. I couldn't wait to start a family and be the best wife a woman could be." She sighed. "Sometimes things just aren't meant to be. That love haunts me and makes me wish for things I can't have. I keep telling myself to count my blessings and to stop longing for the past. I tried to move on, but I made a mess of it all. I didn't take enough time to get to know Richard. It never occurred to me to ask if he already had a wife. Once he's out of my life for good, I'll start again.

We both know I'll never be able to pay you, so I'll find a widower. I won't be your problem any longer. I can work as hard as anyone, and I know ranch work. I think I could be an asset to the right man. I just won't be able to go to the barn raising and take a gander at the men who might need help. I know I'm no prize, and I don't want you to feel sorry for me. We were very close once... but that was forever ago."

It hurt to hear her talk. Didn't she look in the mirror and see that she was still lovely? Didn't she know that her goodness shone brightly within her? Mostly she should know that what they had wasn't forever ago. Now wasn't the time to tell her that, though. She'd think he only felt pity for her.

"Do you have another dress you could wear to the barn raising? If you're going to take your time getting to know the widowers, you might as well see them all in one place to compare a bit." He wanted to bite his tongue. But he needed to get her to trust that he'd never hurt her the way Richard had.

"I do."

"Then come home with me, and tomorrow we'll all go to the barn raising. I'm not leaving you here." He expected her to stiffen, but she sighed instead.

"I suppose that would be for the best but how do I know I still have any dresses left? Your brothers don't like me and at least one of them must hate me. I just wish..." She sounded deflated.

"What do you wish?"

"I wish that we could go back in time. I'm not sure if I could have done anything that would have made a difference, but... never mind. I was thinking if I told you the truth things might be different, but if I had you'd be dead. My father wasn't kidding about killing you. You were my best friend, and I missed you so."

"I missed you too. I was remembering when you named

the cow Bennie and I told you it had to be a girl's name. You didn't talk to me for over a week. Let's get back and we'll check on your clothes. I know my brothers were upset about what happened. But I don't know a one of them that would have cut up your dress. I'll check and see if anyone saw anything."

CHAPTER SIX

*D*olly drove the wagon, and all the Kavanagh men rode their horses. Gemma was nervous and so glad Dolly was accompanying her. According to Dolly, she'd never missed a barn raising. She said the dancing was the best part. She was friendly with most of the women, but since she worked for Kavanaghs a few looked down on her a bit.

"It wasn't like this in the years before the war. A good housekeeper was worth her weight in gold. The wives all helped their husbands and families to make their ranches or farms prosper and they all knew how to be kind and generous to one another. I don't know if it's because the town has grown or if we have more women used to being waited on, but it has changed. I pay little attention to it all. I'm happy, and I'm doing what I love. I love all those boys as if they were mine. I'm proud of them most of the time, but that's the way it is with boys." She gave a hearty laugh. "Listen to me going on about boys. I know they're grown men, but to me they will always be my boys."

"They love you, Dolly. I can see it in their eyes when they

look at you. They actually do as you ask. I've lived in this community most of my life and it's true what you've said. People lived and let live. We all worshiped together every Sunday. All of us, sinners and those who pretended to not know sin." Gemma laughed. "Many of the friends I had moved long ago it seems. I'm not sure but I felt a cooling of friendships when I was still in school. Now with the fiasco of my not-real marriage, I've felt a coldness close to freezing coming from the townspeople. Thank you for standing by me, Dolly."

"No thanks needed. I happen to really like you. I bet pre-sliced pie becomes all the rage." She gave Gemma a sidelong look and laughed. Dolly reached out and patted Gemma's hand. "I'm upset about this whole business too, but I'm not buying the intruder theory. I expect you'll be getting an apology soon."

"I don't want to cause any trouble."

"You couldn't be trouble if you tried. Well, you do have a certain someone in knots, but other than that…"

"Teagan will make sure I'm introduced to widowers today. I think it's time for me to marry. I need the protection and stability being married will give me."

"Hasn't Teagan been protecting you and providing for you? Look all you want, but don't forget to look at the man closest to you." Dolly pulled back on the reins, and the wagon stopped.

Teagan was at Gemma's side in an instant, waiting to help her down. After taking a deep breath she leaned into his welcoming embrace as she put her hands on his broad shoulders. His lingering hands warmed her and frightened her, both.

"You look fetching in blue. I'm glad you came."

"I do need to get me a husband."

He frowned. "What exactly is your reasoning for having to marry in such a hurry?"

"Teagan!" shouted one of his brothers. Then the rest of the Kavanaghs were all calling to him to get to work.

"Save a dance for me!" he told her.

She watched him walk away. He would break her heart, and she wasn't sure she could do it again, to either of them. He'd see she wasn't welcomed in the community and that would change his mind. There were young women gathered and staring openly at the Kavanagh brothers. He'd find a good woman soon.

She hurried to the back of the wagon and began to unload her pies. She drew many strange glances, but she didn't care. They didn't have to eat her pie. She had brought her sewing with her in case she was left on her own.

But Dolly was standing with a circle of women and waved at her to join them. She stood straight and tall as she made her way to them. Dolly made room for her and smiled. "This is my friend, Gemma."

"Gemma what last name are you going by? The fake husband's last name or your given name?"

Her heart jumped. It was starting already. "Thank you for asking, Jenny. I'm going by Maguire since Mr. Parks tricked me into marriage."

"It wasn't a marriage though. You were just living with that man. You never once guessed he had another wife? I would think one would have realized the truth." Jenny tried to look innocent, but she was certainly flaming the fires.

Gemma put her hand over her heart. "To my everlasting shame, it never occurred to me. I should have waited a bit before getting married. I thought I knew him, but I didn't know him at all. I was tired of soldiers coming onto my property and of being scared to death. I foolishly thought a husband would fix all that. Most of you know my mother had just died and my father never came home from the war. I scraped by for years to pay off the land and then for money for taxes, but I was proud of the fact that I was able to keep that land. Imagine my distress when I learned that Mr. Parks was a lying, thieving, man who not only brought me incredible shame but ran off after apparently mortgaging all I owned! Then someone emptied my home of all my possessions. They didn't even leave me my clothes. I didn't know what I would do, but Dolly and the Kavanaghs welcomed me onto their ranch. I'm not sure what to do next. It's been an incredibly hard time."

"I heard that Mr. Parks is still in the area," a rancher's wife, Ellen, said. "You poor thing. Your story breaks my heart."

Gemma quickly glanced at Jenny and was glad to see her outrage.

"Thank you, Ellen, I appreciate your kind words." Most of the women in the circle nodded.

Finally, she could breathe and not be expected to hang her head in shame.

The afternoon went by quickly, and before she knew it, she was helping to serve the supper. More than one woman commented on the efficiency of the already sliced pies. Gemma couldn't help but smile.

"I'm glad you're having a good time."

Gemma gazed at Teagan's honest face. "Thank you. I was so nervous coming here. Dolly was of great help to me, and I think they might actually like me."

"What's not to like? I'm not making light of it. I know you've had a hard time. I'm glad things are changing." He smiled until her face heated unbearably. After a bit, he walked away and found a space on a bench to sit.

He confused her at every turn. He promised to introduce her to a few widowers yet the way he grinned at her made her almost forget about anything but him.

Dolly was the one who introduced her first to Cal Meagher, the host of the raising and widower with six sons. Gemma smiled and thanked him for such a pleasant day.

"There will be dancing later. Save one for me?" His coffee-brown eyes showed kindness within. He also looked exhausted. Was it from the busy day or from taking care of the boys? "If you'll excuse me? My sons are wrestling with some younger boys and I hear yells of pain." Hurriedly he tipped his hat before he raced to the boys.

"He's a very busy man," Dolly observed.

"Yes, he could certainly use some help around here."

Dolly chuckled. "Let's see who else is here before you decide on the first man you meet."

Next, she was introduced to Ed Calver. He had hard black eyes and his gray hair looked unwashed.

"I've heard of you, Miss. Maguire. You're prettier than you were described. I'm sorry for all your troubles. I've had enough of my own to last a lifetime. I wish you well." He turned and walked away.

Insulted, nicely but still he'd insulted her. He wanted nothing to do with her, which was fine.

Dolly shrugged. "He's too old for you. Come."

"Adam Johnson, this is my friend, Gemma Maguire."

Adam smiled. "Yes, Gemma, I remember you from school. You always had the correct answer if I recall correctly."

"It's nice to see you again, Adam. I remember you pulling my hair," she said with a laugh.

"It's good to see you. So many we knew back then have gone. I have to confess I listened when others spoke of you. I'm so sorry you've had a hard time. I liked your parents, and I'm sorry for your loss." He looked down and took his one-year-old daughter from his oldest son.

"Thank you, Eddie."

He gave his baby a kiss on her cheek and she smiled and then put her head down on his broad shoulder. "I have four children. Their ma died birthing this one." He patted the baby's back.

"It must be hard to work your ranch." Gemma liked the way he was so sweet to his daughter.

"It is. I wish I could steal Dolly here to keep house for me."

Dolly smiled. "You'll find yourself a sweet wife soon enough I expect."

"I don't have any love to give a woman. Not now and possibly never."

"Perfectly understandable," Gemma said as she gazed at the blond-haired, blue eyed man.

"I need to put her down for her nap. If I'm still here for the dancing, I'd love it if both of you saved a dance for me." He nodded and left.

"His heart is taken." Gemma sighed.

"So, he says. You never know, he glowed talking about knowing you from your school days. You know, you don't have to limit yourself to widowers, you've been accepted by many in the community."

"Perhaps but they might expect... relations. That is my only condition. I don't want to be touched."

"There's John Dew. Let's walk in his direction."

Gemma followed Dolly. Somehow, she had thought it would be easier. She hadn't thought about the fact that they'd loved their dead wives. Just because she wanted to have her supposed husband in jail...

"This is John Dew. John, this is Gemma Maguire."

John nodded. Poor man, he looked downright done in.

"I heard you were husband hunting, Miss. Maguire. I'd like to put my name in for your consideration. It's taking everything I've got trying to keep things together for the sake of the children, but I'm drowning. I never knew how much my dear Nancy did."

He could have used a haircut, but he kept his beard nicely trimmed. Gemma bet he had smiled a lot when his wife was alive. He might just be the one.

"How many children do you have Mr. Dew?"

"Call me John. I have five. Three boys and two girls. Ages run from three to seven. Do you like children, Gemma?"

"I do, I know little about taking care of them, I must confess, but it was always my dream to have a family. Tell me about your place."

Dolly quietly ducked out and walked to a group of women.

"It was a grand place, but it needs a lot of work to even be called decent. I was making some headway, but things just kind of fell apart. I know you have had bad things happen to you and so have I. Truthfully, I was hoping to meet you today to see if we would suit. I know I can make the ranch profitable again. I just need time to do it. Look at me telling you all my troubles on our first meeting. My children are resting under that tree if you'd like to meet them." His eyes were filled with hope.

"Of course." She walked with him to the two quilts laid side by side. They all had dark hair and blue eyes like their father except for the youngest. Her hair was strawberry blond, and her blue eyes were darker than the rest.

"Children, this is Miss. Gemma. My eldest i Lorna, she's seven but she does so much more than a wee seven-year-old. Next is John Junior. He is six years old and a strong lad. This is Clark and my other son is Martin. The little babe is Aubrey. She's but three years old."

"It's very nice to meet all of you," Gemma said gently. The children seemed rather stiff but well behaved.

"It's nice to meet you too, Miss. Gemma," Lorna replied politely.

"Are you gonna be our new ma?" Clark asked. John Junior jabbed Clark in the side with his elbow. Clark gave John Junior the look of the devil.

"Clark, I've just met Miss. Gemma." John said.

"How long does it take?" Clark asked, sounding very impatient.

"Sometimes it can take a while for two people to see if they are right for one another," Gemma answered.

"I thought we were here to catch us a ma, right Martin?"

John turned red and shuffled his feet. "You may play if you like, but keep an eye on each other."

Clark was off and running with all but Lorna and Aubrey. Lorna watched the rest with a look of longing on her face. It tugged at Gemma's heart. She reached down and picked up Aubrey. "I can watch her for a little bit so Lorna can play too."

Lorna gave her the biggest smile and then looked at her pa. He nodded, and she was running across the field with the others.

"That's a mighty nice thing you just did, Gemma. Lorna hardly ever gets time to be a child. Thank you." He had a slight mist in his eyes. "Will you be fine with Aubrey? I have a barn to help finish."

"I'll be fine. Plus there are many women here, so I'm sure I'll get a lot of advice, wanted or not."

He chuckled. "I do believe you're right."

Aubrey must have been half asleep when Gemma first held her; when they were alone, she pushed to get out of Gemma's arms and began screaming.

Dolly hurried over. "Hush Aubrey, you'll scare Miss. Gemma."

Aubrey stared at Dolly and then at Gemma. She suddenly

smiled and reached for a piece of Gemma's hair and pulled it. Gemma tried to pretend it didn't hurt, but they had a heck of a time getting Aubrey to let go.

"What are you doing with this child?" Dolly asked.

"I felt bad for Lorna. It seemed to me all she got to do was watch the children."

"You have a soft heart, Gemma," a male voice behind her murmured. She grew warm. Teagan was behind her.

She turned and Aubrey launched herself out of Gemma's arms and into Teagan's. Aubrey sighed in contentment and put her thumb in her mouth before she lay her head on his chest.

Gemma's lips twitched at the amazed look on Teagan's face. "I didn't know you had such a way with children."

"It's not just children, look around at all the women who now want me as their husband."

She turned this way and then the other way. "Oh my, they're looking at you like you're a prized—bull."

He laughed. "I thought for sure you were going to say pig."

"I was," she confessed, giving him her sassiest grin.

"Any ideas what I should do with this girl?"

"No, she looks content. Don't you think so Dolly?"

Dolly's eyes widened. "Don't try to get me on the wrong end of Teagan. But she does look blissful."

"I'll take her," a well-dressed young woman said as she practically pressed herself against Teagan to get Aubrey. "I'm Lisa Andies. Your daughter is beautiful; she looks just like you." She shifted the girl in her arms. "What's her name?" Lisa never once took her gaze from Teagan.

"Nice to meet you, Miss. Andies. You are holding Aubrey and while she *is* beautiful, she doesn't belong to me. I was helping Miss. Maguire with her."

"You're the nanny?" Lisa immediately shoved Aubrey back into Gemma's arms.

"My word! Gemma is no nanny. She is just a sweet woman doing a favor." Dolly turned her back on Lisa. "Come, Gemma, we can go sit over there. The ladies there are forever missing their grandchildren. We could both learn a few tips on child rearing." She led Gemma to a table that had been moved under a tree.

Dolly laughed. "Teagan will get rid of her. He always does. You know he hasn't shown any interest in anyone except for you."

"We're just friends." Gemma sat down and the other women immediately admired Aubrey.

Later the men put the tools away and John came and got his daughter. He graciously thanked all the women and gave Gemma and extra-long smile.

"Save a dance for me, don't forget."

CHAPTER SEVEN

*T*eagan gritted his teeth. He'd spent the last few hours watching Gemma meet the widowers. It looked as though John Dew was the winner, and Teagan was irritated to no end.

"I'm surprised you didn't hit your thumb with the hammer with all the staring you've been doing." Sullivan gave him a wide grin. "I haven't seen you this interested in anything except for bulls in a long time. Are you going to dance with her? I'll be happy to take your turn if you like. I can tell her you have a weak ankle or something."

Teagan shook his head and chuckled. "I can take my own turn, brother. There are women here you could dance with."

"I suppose but none so pretty as Gemma. I'm glad you two are friends again. So, which lucky lady do you think I should ask first?"

"There aren't too many of our age. They seem to be older or too young. But there are plenty who dance."

"I noticed the same thing. I'm going to go by dress color. I will start with green."

"That's a new way. It almost makes sense."

"Teagan I always make sense. The fiddle is playing. Let's go." Sullivan quickened his walk and Teagan shook his head. Maybe blue dresses would be the way to start.

He almost groaned when he saw Gemma dancing with Adam Johnson. Adam had that one-year-old to entice Gemma with. He was a nice man too. There didn't seem to be much spark, but the baby was a very heavy draw.

Lisa was suddenly standing in front of him. If he'd been paying attention, he could have avoided her.

"May I have this dance?"

She smiled like it was a great surprise. "I'd love to."

A clingier woman he'd never danced with. He'd put a bit distance between them, but she found ways to press against him. He glanced up and saw Gemma starring daggers at him. He smiled at her, and she turned away.

So, she was jealous. Good, maybe she'd realize his worth. He frowned. He didn't want that, did he? Part of him was attracted to her but he couldn't get past her betrayal. It still made little sense to him. Pieces of her story were either missing, or she'd lied. Besides, he would have a true marriage when he got married. She didn't want to marry him; he didn't already have children.

The song was finally over, and he disentangled himself. He glanced at her dress. Violet. No more violet dresses for him tonight. He gave her a short quick bow and didn't escort her back to wherever she came from. He had a feeling he'd be hiding from her before the night was through.

He glanced at the people dancing to the next song and Gemma was in Cal Meagher's arms. Cal had a newborn. This was not playing fair. He watched and they talked at great length. He'd dance with her the next dance.

But that wasn't to be. She was now dancing with John Dew. Enough was enough. He could no longer stand there, so he went in search of the whiskey. He refused to watch her all night.

Ten minutes later, he was watching her with a shot of whiskey in his hand.

"You got it bad," Quinn teased.

"You don't have to rub it in. Have you heard anything more about her dress?"

"No, and we can't even come up with a suspect. Someone apparently has an innocent act down."

"We'll get to the bottom it."

"Teagan?" Gemma stood before him looking hopeful. "Would you mind awfully dancing with me?"

"I told you to save me a dance, and it seems you have." He handed Quinn his whiskey and took Gemma's hand then led her to the dancing and pulled her into his arms. She should have been his years ago. She fit him as no one else did or ever would. He brought her in closer than he probably should have, but he couldn't help himself.

"You look lovely, Gemma. I'm glad you decided to come. Everyone wants to dance with you. I've seen you in one man's arms after another." She stiffened. "I didn't mean it that way. I guess I didn't enjoy having to wait for my turn to dance with you. Have you decided?"

She gazed into his eyes. "No, John wants to court me but doesn't have the time, so I offered to come out next week and cook dinner for them all. None of them want a wife, and I thought that was what I wanted, but I also want friendship and a bit of affection."

He smiled. "Feel how nice it is in my arms?"

"But—"

"Shh, feel and let the moment linger. There is a spark I only experience when you are near. Do you feel it too?"

Confusion crossed her face. "I don't understand." She let go of him and walked away.

She experienced the spark too… he knew it.

WHEN THE NIGHT ended and they were back at the ranch, Gemma walked out onto the wrap-around porch. She stood in the shadows.

Please God, I'm lost and alone. I know not what to do. I need your guidance more now than ever. I've only loved one man, but I don't think he truly loves me. His pride was hurt, and I think he's trying to redeem it. It's not meanness… it's just misguided feelings. Lord, I long for his love, I see him in my dreams. He's with me in my heart always, and I don't want to be tempted into making a mistake. He deserves more than the trouble of me. Amen.

A cloud passed in front of the full moon, and she allowed a tear to fall in the darkness. Teagan had loved his parents, and the truth would put that in jeopardy. A man should hold on to his happy memories of his mother and father. No, the secret would only tear the family apart and she couldn't do that even if it meant she had to walk away from Teagan forever.

With a heavy heart, she went back inside and up to her room. Someone had filled a vase with yellow roses and set it on her bedside table. She picked the vase up and smelled the flowers. They soothed her and she was grateful. After setting them back down, she got changed. She had sewn granny gowns, but she put ribbon bows on each. A small one at the top front. They made her feel pretty.

She climbed into bed and leaned over to turn the oil lamp off, but a knock at the door stopped her. Before she uttered a word, the door exploded inward, and Brogan rushed in and closed the door behind him.

"You are to stay away from my brother. I thought we had this conversation before, but I saw the way you looked at him while you danced with him. You will not lead him on the path of despair. No matter what. Evidently, you don't get the hint you're not wanted here. Unless you crave pity, because that is all there is for you here. I'll use every penny I have and buy you furniture so you can go home. I'll expect an announcement of you leaving in the morning." He practically growled each word. It was obvious now who had cut her dress and bonnet.

Her eyes burned while he stared mulishly at her. She leaned over and turned the lamp off. She lay down with her back to him waiting for him to leave. It seemed to take forever, but she finally heard the door open and close.

That settled it. She would marry John Dew. Teagan might hold the loan on her property but there was something not right about the whole thing. She couldn't count on that land ever being hers again. She bet Brogan would be happy to let John know that tomorrow she'd be by to cook supper for the family.

What was she supposed to do with the love she held in her heart? She was an adult. She sighed heavily. She'd have to live with it. No one ever said she'd be happy. Once she heard her mother tell her she'd grow up to be a happy young woman. But then she started to say no one owed her happiness and it would behoove her to remember that. Her poor mother. Gemma never walked in her shoes so she couldn't judge. That was for God to do. What had happened when her ma stood in front of God? Did He tell her how sinful she'd been? Maybe her mother had asked for forgiveness before she died. Could you ask after you died? Would God be merciful? What if she wasn't sorry and hadn't asked for forgiveness? Her thoughts went round and round. She'd read the Bible in the morning. Maybe she would find some answers.

But she couldn't sleep. *Jesus died for our sins. God is a*

forgiving God. Doesn't God know our hearts? Her mother broke her marriage vows and paid a price for it every day of her life. She stayed away from the man, but Gemma had a feeling her mother had always loved that man. Would giving in to temptation be forgiven if she asked for forgiveness and never did it again? How did one stop loving another?

Would it be the same if she married one man while loving another? Was that a sin if she stayed true to her husband? She had to believe that God was all knowing and forgiving. Her mother was in heaven, wasn't she? Gemma refused to think she wasn't. It would be too unbearable to contemplate.

People made mistakes every day. In the Bible God commanded forgiveness.

Gemma closed her eyes, and her last thought was of her mother. Was she in heaven or not?

"You're going where?" Teagan asked as he narrowed his eyes.

"I will cook for the Dews today. It didn't look as though they'd had a good meal in a very long time. Would it be fine if I took some food with me?" She tried to smile, but she wasn't in the mood.

"Did you sleep last night? Your eyes have circles under them."

She glanced away. "I tossed and turned for a long while. I'm fine, though."

"Does John know you're coming? Did you make plans yesterday?"

She shook her head still avoiding his gaze. "Brogan went to tell him."

"What does Brogan have to do with this?"

She looked at him. "He came to my room last night. He

72

doesn't want me here, and he's just hurrying the inevitable. I'm mortified to know you all pity me. I need a home. No matter where I go lately, it's been wrong, and I need to find the right one. I know the children will be a lot of work, but once I get a routine, it'll be fine. It'll keep me busy and not dwelling."

He was staring at her, his jaw clenched. "Brogan came to your room last night? Were you in bed?"

"Yes, I had just gotten in but had yet to turn the lamp off."

"Is John the man you have your heart set on?"

There were tears in her eyes before she turned away. "I have learned my heart doesn't matter. A good man who won't make a fool of me is what I need. I doubt he'll want more children. It'll be just perfect."

"You don't sound very convincing."

She sighed and gazed at him, a sad smile on her face. "I don't suppose I do. When I married Richard, I was plain stupid, but the men in the area were trying to take my land and unless I wanted to shoot them all, I thought I should get married. Funny how the man I picked to save me was the one who took everything from me, including my pride and confidence. Do what you have to so you can survive."

"Does he know he won't be allowed to touch you?" His voice was more sarcastic than he planned.

Shaking her head, she lifted her skirt just enough so she could run. The look on her face made him wince. He'd made fun of her secret terror.

He started to go after her, but he saw Brogan riding in. Teagan hurried out the front door and to the barn.

"Brogan, I think we have a few things to straighten out."

"I don't think so," Brogan said as he pushed past Teagan.

"I know we do! Just who do you think you are? You tore the dress up, didn't you?"

Brogan shrugged his right shoulder. "So, what if I did? I'm

just doing you a favor. She tore your heart out once, and Ma was always saying that Gemma's ma was a no-good whore. Gemma must be like her mother. We don't need her kind living here!"

"Ma said that about Mrs. Maguire? I never heard it." He shook his head. "It doesn't matter anyway. How could you have treated Gemma that way? She is sweet and gentle. She has beauty both inside and out and when she looks at me… never mind. I don't want you trying to get her off the ranch. That is *her* decision."

"She's taking her sweet time. I'm just pushing toward the inevitable!" Brogan shook his head and stomped away.

What was going on with Brogan? He'd best adjust his attitude. His hostility toward Gemma made no sense. If anyone should bear grudges it should be Teagan. His brother had always been easy going until… no, it was after he got back from the war. Just when Brogan had become bitter, Teagan wasn't sure. Getting the ranch back up and running had taken all his time, and he still had a lot to do. Had he pushed his brothers too hard? Maybe they all wanted an equal say.

His father hadn't wanted it that way. The eldest was in charge. Maybe he should ask for their input. He ran his fingers through his hair. Maybe Sullivan knew what was wrong with Brogan.

He asked Dolly to bring him coffee into his office. He had plenty of work to do.

A few hours later, he heard Gemma asking Dolly advice about children and what they liked to eat. He shook his head. She was still going out there. He pushed away from his desk and went into the kitchen.

"Still planning to go?" He tried to keep his voice as neutral as possible.

"Yes. I want to get there early to get to know the children.

A seven-year-old shouldn't have the responsibility of taking care of the house and the other children. I just want to help."

He could tell she thought she meant what she said. He believed she wanted to help, but would it bring her a happy life? He sure didn't think so.

"I'd be happy to drive the wagon out there for you."

"Teagan, that is nice but I can drive. I know you have a lot of work to do, and I want nothing I do to interfere with ranch life." The smile she gave him was so sweet he wanted to grab her up and tell her not to go, but he wouldn't win her back if he took that approach.

"I'll have someone hitch it all up for you."

"Thank you, Teagan, I appreciate it."

"No problem. Try to leave to come back before dark. The roads aren't easy to navigate in the dark." He waited for her to nod then he left.

One day with those kids would make anyone crazy. How John got them to be well behaved at the barn raising he had no idea.

CHAPTER EIGHT

*G*emma slowed the horses to a stop before she had to turn onto John's property. She patted her hair and brushed all the dust from her dress. *It'll be a good day.* She flicked the lines, and the horses started again.

The house wasn't falling apart. It needed a bit of care, but it was far better than her house had been. As soon as she pulled up, she set the brake and wrapped the lines around it. Standing she started to climb down. Where was John? She knocked on the door and heard a big commotion.

She opened the door and was horrified by the condition she found inside. There wasn't one clean place to stand. Lorna looked surprised, while John Junior sat at the table doing nothing. The three others were running through the house throwing what looked like porridge at each other.

Gemma was speechless. "What's going on?"

Lorna shrugged. "The usual. John won't help, and the others won't listen to me. Pa will be mad at me when he gets home."

"What if I helped you out today and we all clean?"

"Really?" Hope brightened her face. "I would like that."

"Have you had breakfast?" Gemma already guessed they had porridge.

"Yes."

"John, take Clark, Martin, and Aubrey out to the water pump and help them wash. Bring soap and a towel with you."

She held the door open until they filed out. Looking around the room, she wondered where to start. The look on Lorna's face was so sorrowful.

"Listen, honey, this is not your fault. You have too much to do. Does John Junior help at all?"

Lorna shook her head. "He thinks because he's a boy he doesn't have to help. I just don't know what to do anymore. When Pa comes home and the house looks like this, I can see the disappointment in his face, and that makes me feel really bad."

"We'll have John Junior haul some buckets of water, and we'll all work together to get this place clean. I bet we can even find something for little Aubrey to do. How does that sound?"

Lorna smiled. "That sounds like a fine idea."

It took a lot of long hard work to get the house in order. They scraped plenty of porridge off the floors and the walls. John Junior thought he was going to sit and watch, but Gemma soon told him the way of things. After the house was clean, Gemma showed Lorna how to make stew and how to bake biscuits.

There were plenty of dirty diapers, and Gemma put them into a giant washtub and poured hot water they heated on the stove over them. She wasn't sure at what age children no longer use diapers. She really didn't know much about children. But she was able to get Aubrey, Martin, and Clark all down for their naps.

After that Gemma took Lorna and John Junior outside

and led them to a spot under a big oak tree where she had them sit down.

"I know it must be tough with your ma gone, and there is a lot of work that needs to be done each day. John Junior, Lorna can't do this all by herself, she needs your help. While she is the oldest and is in charge, you are the man of the family when your father's not here. It's your job to look after the little ones and make sure they're safe and not making messes. We'll have to figure out how to split the work so it's fair. I bet it will make your Pa very happy."

John Dew rode toward them and when he saw her, he smiled. He reined in his horse and slid out of the saddle. "Well this is a nice surprise. I didn't expect you today."

"Brogan said he would come over and let you know I was coming. I guess he forgot."

John looked at the two children. "I hope you two haven't been given Miss. Gemma any trouble."

Gemma smiled. "Wait until you see all the work they've done. The house is so clean, and Lorna's been busy cooking. The other three are taking naps."

John's eyes widened. "Well this I'll have to see."

Lorna took her father's hand and led him inside. She blushed with pride when her father whistled.

"I'd forgotten the house could look this good. Gemma, you made such a difference in just a few hours. I thank you."

Gemma shook her head. "It wasn't me. It was your children, all of them. Even little Aubrey helped by washing walls. At one point I wasn't sure we would get all the porridge off. It was stuck on pretty good, but we managed. I was just speaking to Lorna and John Junior about splitting up the work in a fair way, so Lorna wasn't left with all of it. I'm hoping you'll work it out. Now if you'll excuse me, I have plenty of diapers to wash. Lorna and John Junior, I'll need your help." She stood at the door again and waited for the children to go back outside before she turned and smiled at John. "You're welcome to help too if you'd like."

John sputtered as if the water he'd just swallowed went down the wrong way. "As much as I enjoy washing diapers, I have stalls to muck out. I do appreciate you being here." He stared into her eyes until she looked away.

Later, Gemma closed the door behind her. Though John was nice, and she had fun with his children, there wasn't a spark. A spark that Teagan had talked about, the spark she felt only with Teagan.

TEAGAN PACED BACK and forth along the front porch. Hadn't he told her to be home before dark? He sighed and stared at the sky. The sun would set soon, and she would barely be able to see where she was going. Had she even started to drive home? He should've gone with her or he should've sent somebody with her or perhaps he should've sent somebody to escort her home. Now he was just plain worried. Anything could happen. There were wild animals out there, not to mention Richard was probably still around, and Texas was still unsettled. She could run into all kinds of trouble. Why did she have to be so doggone independent, anyway?

"You know your pacing will not make her come home any quicker," Dolly said. She handed him a glass with a bit of whiskey splashed into it. "Wait, a few more minutes until it's dark and then go after her."

Teagan rubbed the back of his neck as he tossed back the whiskey. "Yeah, I best wait, or she'll get mad thinking I was keeping track of her. I don't know what John has that I don't have."

"Have you asked her? Have you even told her you're interested? What is she supposed to think? You have men rebuilding her house. She probably thinks as soon as the house is done, you'll pack her up and send her over there. Maybe you should just tell her how you feel."

Teagan put the glass down on the table. He looked up at the sky and then at Dolly. He thought he knew how he felt, but what if he was wrong? What if it was all just one big mistake? What if she didn't feel the same way about him? No, he couldn't take the chance as much as he wanted to. Unless she said it first... that was a different thing altogether. He couldn't picture her professing her love for him. He picked up his hat and was just about to put it on when the sound of horses' hooves could be heard. He took a deep breath. What a relief.

He immediately went to her side and lifted her down. She was filthy from head to toe. "What the heck happened to you? You look like, well I don't even know what you look like. Dolly, do we have enough hot water so Gemma can have a bath?"

Dolly chuckled. "I'm sure I could come up with enough." She went inside.

"Seriously, what happened to you?"

Gemma looked down at her dress and then touched her hair. She stood straight and tall and looked him right in the eye. "I was helping at the Dew place. They've had a hard time of it since their ma died. The place was filthy, and poor Lorna was trying to do it all herself. John Junior thought it was women's work, so he sat in a chair watching Lorna try her best to make sense of the chaos."

"Why do I have the feeling you set him straight?" Teagan smiled at her.

"I set them all straight. I had every one of them working, even the little one. Did you know when porridge hardens on the walls or the floor it's almost impossible to get it off?"

He laughed long and hard and then stopped. He couldn't

remember the last time he laughed like that. "No, I didn't know about the porridge."

She gave him a big smile. "If I hadn't had to scrub it myself, I would never have known either. It was a lot of work, but I had a good time with the children."

"And John?" Teagan took a step toward her. "Did you have a good time with him too?"

She shrugged. "He's a nice man. He's a good man and a good father, but I don't know. I know I said I didn't want any type of love or involvement, but now I'm not so sure. I need to rethink this whole marriage thing. Maybe the best thing for me is to go back to my own ranch alone. Maybe I don't need a husband. I have my rifle, and I can hire a couple men to do the work. I'm sure eventually I'll be able to pay you back."

"But I thought you wanted children. Wasn't that the whole point of finding a widower? You do know how babies are made, right?"

Her mouth opened and then closed as she stared at him. "You act like I'm some silly female who can't make up her mind. I made up my mind years ago, but it was unmade for me by my father, and a lot has happened since then. Yes, I do know how babies are made." She walked away and went into the house.

THE NEXT DAY Gemma was just finishing her coffee when Teagan came into the house. He glanced at her, but she couldn't read his expression. Maybe he was right. Maybe she was some silly female who couldn't make up her mind. She watched as he poured a cup of coffee and leaned against the counter sipping it and staring at her.

"Was there something I can help you with?"

"Not that I know of. Are you going out to see John? Or maybe one of the other widowers?"

She flashed him a look of annoyance. "I thought I'd spend the day here, but if you'd rather I go somewhere else..."

"No, I was just wondering. Actually, I came in to tell you to be careful. Richard has been sighted at your property again. Quinn's over there now with a couple of the men looking around to see if they can figure out what he's up to." He shook his head. "It must be something pretty important, or he'd have moved on by now. Is there a deed to another parcel of land? Or, I don't know, I can't think of what else it could be besides money?"

"Richard never met my father, so whatever he thinks he knows, someone else told him. But obviously he wasn't told where or he wouldn't still be prowling around the property. Did anyone go into town to get the sheriff?"

"Well, here's the thing. Somehow the sheriff thinks you're crazy. The bank owner Victor Lyons has everyone convinced that you don't own the property."

"But you have the papers, don't you? Why don't you show them to him? Richard has no right to be on my property."

"I know, I just don't want to show my hand until I can figure out what Victor Lyons has to do with all this." He set his coffee aside. "Has Brogan given you any more trouble?"

She shook her head. "I haven't even seen him yet this morning. I'm just gonna try to stay out of his way. He doesn't like me for some reason, and I don't think he'd tell me the truth if I ask why."

He stared at her and smiled.

"Why are you staring at me that way?" Her face heated, and she was tempted to turn away but there was something in his eyes that prevented her.

"I was thinking you don't look at all different from when we were kids. You still have that impish grin I always liked."

The mild flirtation sent her heart fluttering. She looked away and changed the subject. "I do need a favor. I would like to harvest my garden, but I don't want to go alone. Could you send one of your men with me?"

He frowned and shook his head. "Didn't you just hear me tell you that Richard was near there? I wouldn't feel right sending you. It's just not safe. Do you think your garden can wait a few more days? If so, I'll take you myself."

"If that's what it takes to get into my garden, I can wait. I wish… I wish I never met Richard. I've wished that so many times, but there's nothing I can do about it. I try to put it all out of my mind, but I'm constantly reminded of him. Partly because he's been showing up, which is bad enough, but the worst is when someone tries to touch me. Even the most innocent touch makes me cringe. I keep trying not to react like that. I tell myself this is not Richard, but it doesn't seem to do any good. I guess I just don't want to end up alone. Maybe I should give John and his kids a chance."

Teagan almost looked as if he was in a panic. "What if we practice hugging? That might be of some help to you."

"Practice hugging? Really? I don't think that will work."

"We can try. We've known each other since we were children, and I know you trust me." He stepped forward to where she was sitting and offered her his hand. She hesitated for a moment and then put her hand in his. She got to her feet, and they were standing closer than she thought they'd be. For a moment, she wanted to back away, but she didn't.

Teagan gently pulled her into his arms, and she tried taking deep breaths to calm herself. She knew she was as stiff as a board, but she couldn't help it. It was the fear of being hurt the fear of the pain and humiliation that kept her from leaning into him. He pulled her closer and kissed her on the cheek and then let her go.

"Now that wasn't so bad, was it?" he asked with a note of

tenderness in his voice.

"It wasn't good… but you're right, it wasn't so bad." She shook her head, feeling helpless. "I just hate for you to spend your time on me and not have it work. I don't think John expects hugs and kisses from me."

"You might be right for now. Initially he won't expect any intimacy, but as years go on don't you think he'll want you to ask to act like a wife? I'm not saying this to scare you. I'm just saying the truth of things." His smile seemed sad. "But if you're set on having John, you must tell him he won't be able to touch you."

"Would I even have to say a word about it?" She frowned.

"What about after the wedding? What about holding hands on your wedding day? You have to touch him when he escorts you into church. But you can probably handle that, right?" He stepped back and gazed into her eyes.

He definitely made her feel uncomfortable, and she didn't like it, but he was right. Her shoulders slumped, and she looked away from him. "I keep thinking of these big dreams of what my life might be like or what I'd like it to be but I'm only fooling myself. I'll never be normal and the sooner I accept it the better. At one time I thought about moving to a different town but that wouldn't solve anything. As soon as we finish this thing with Richard, I'll go back to my ranch."

"I didn't come in here to shatter your dreams or make you unhappy. I'm sorry it ended up that way."

"I just feel sorry for John and his children. They don't deserve the hardship they're going through and if I can help…"

"Helping is always good, but in the end, I don't think it will be helping. Children can sense things, and they'll know there's something wrong between you and their father. But you know that's between you and John. I don't know why I am spouting off advice. You don't see me married with children. Most days I'm not even happy. I just hate to see you sad."

She gave him a small smile. "Thank you for being a friend. Well, if I can't do my garden I might as well do yours." She turned and grabbed a straw hat.

"Are we? Are we even friends?"

Gemma whirled around to face him again. "How can you even ask? Unless you don't want to be friends with me. I know I've been nothing but a bother lately, and if you'd really cared you would have found a way to stop by when you got back from the war. If anyone had cared they could have stopped by, but no one did. So now I guess we aren't even friends. In fact, I guess I don't have any friends." Her eyes watered, and she quickly hurried outside.

She picked up the basket and headed to the garden feeling as low as a person could be. She kneeled in the dirt and bent her head downward.

Please Lord please fill my heart. It's feeling a bit empty right now. Am I hard to get along with? Am I too opinionated? Do I talk too much? I guess I'm just hurt. You're the only One I have to talk to. I thought Teagan was my friend, and actually he means more to me than just a friend. I guess he didn't, or I didn't... He had to ask if we were friends. I've always heard that when one door closes another opens. I've also heard You provide us with a path of life. But for the life of me I can't find the door or the path. I need help, and if there's any way You could help me figure this all out, I'd be grateful. Not that I'm ungrateful. I mean I have a roof over my head I have food to eat I don't have as many worries as I did. I just don't know where I fit. I wish I knew why everything has to be so difficult for me. I know I'll get through it with Your help. Just sometimes it's so hard. Thank you.

She busied herself weeding the garden picking all the carrots and onions. There were still some green beans lingering, and she picked all those. She left the potatoes for last, but some tomatoes were overripe. Her basket was getting full and very heavy. She stood and wiped her brow, lifted the basket and headed for the house. She had more than enough food for supper.

She walked into the quiet house and looked around. An uneasy feeling fell over her, and she didn't know why. She shivered. Nothing was out of place. She went into the kitchen and put on an apron. She started chopping vegetables putting them into a big cast-iron pot that was already full of boiling water.

She heard a noise and tilted her head trying to figure out where it had come from, but all was quiet. Perhaps she had imagined it. She went to the pantry to retrieve some salt, and the next thing she knew she was on the floor with Richard on top of her. He had a big butcher knife in his hand and his eyes had a wild look about them.

She froze, not daring to scream. She just looked at him, wondering what came next.

"Unless you want me to kill you here, you will get up and walk out of the house with me." His menacing voice sent chills up her spine. Her body shook as she stood and went out the back door with him behind her. Every so often, he jabbed the knife into her back.

"Richard, where are you taking me?" Gemma asked in a whisper.

"I told you be quiet. You're still my wife. I can take you anywhere I want, and there's nothing you can say about it." He shoved her to keep her moving faster.

She had so many questions she wanted to ask, but fear kept her silent. They'd have to wait until they got to where they were going, and from the direction they were heading, it wasn't to her ranch. She didn't dare stop. He'd put that knife through her for sure. She stumbled a few times, eliciting a few snarls from Richard, but there wasn't a marked path and it was hard going. Was this it? Was this the time he would kill her? Why hadn't she left on better terms with Teagan? Why hadn't she just told the secret their families shared? Sure, she had promised her mother, but her mother was dead.

As soon as they were far enough away from anyone, she slowed down a bit. "Can you just tell me what it is you're looking for? I know you've been searching the ranch, but I don't have a clue what's supposed to be there."

"You really don't know much about your pa, do you?" Richard let loose with a harsh laugh. "He was one of the best stagecoach robbers in history. There was gold, a lot of gold in the last job he did. He had it, and it's never been found."

"It's never been found because my father did not rob stagecoaches. He was a rancher."

"Why do you think I came to this dirt-poor town? It certainly wasn't to marry *you,* but that was the only way I could get on your property long enough to search it. I like my women a bit more friendly and a little curvier. I have to tell you, you weren't a very good wife. You'd just lie there weeping and a wailing. It got to be I couldn't stand being around you." More laughter. "You should have seen the look on your face when you found out I had a wife already. Yeah, that look made it all worthwhile except I never found my gold. Now I want you to tell me where it is, and I want you to tell me quick. I don't have time for fooling."

What could she do? Even if she knew anything about gold, if she told him, that would be the end of her. And if she kept insisting that she didn't know and he believed her, that also might end her life. A shudder rippled along her spine.

They walked until they came upon his campsite. He told her to sit down against the tree and there he tied her up with her hands behind her back. Her hopes of being found were very dim. Well, she'd be the talk of the town again, that was for sure. She wanted to be remembered fondly, but there would always be a question about her honesty and her integrity. All she hoped was that he didn't try to touch her that evening.

She strained against the ropes and struggled not to show any emotion when they gave ever so slightly.

Richard had not thought far enough ahead to bring any food with him. He was grouchy as an old bear, and he had that knife, so her only hope was to keep as calm as possible. He hadn't made a fire either, but that was okay. She didn't care since it was still warm in the evenings.

She waited and waited for him to fall asleep, little by little working her hands free. It was the longest wait she could remember. After hours passed, she heard his even snores.

Unfortunately, the moon wasn't full, and it was hard to see. She moved as slowly and silently as she could. Fear embraced her with every breath she took, but she walked away without looking back. At first, she walked very slowly, fearful of making any noise in case she fell. But as she got farther and farther away, she increased her speed.

Then she heard a noise behind her, and a sense of dread shrouded her. Would he take the knife to her this time and kill her? Or just torture her? She hid behind a tree and prayed.

She hadn't realized she was holding her breath until she saw Teagan walk by. "Teagan," she hissed urgently.

He turned in all directions as though trying to find where the voice came from.

Gemma stood and stepped out from behind the tree with tears burning in her eyes. The next thing she knew, she was in his arms and she was embracing him back. He rubbed his hand up and down her back, and she laid her head on his chest taking all the comfort he was offering.

"It was Richard. He kidnapped me, but I got away. He's

either not too far behind me or still sleeping, and I don't know which. He has some crazy story about my father and some gold he stole. Can we just go home now?"

Teagan nodded and let go of her then made some motion with his hand. Before she knew it, several men came out of the woods toward them. His brothers.

"Is he alone?"

"Yes, but he has a butcher knife, his two six-shooters, and a rifle. There is no fire, and it's west of here. I didn't walk a straight line. It's so dark."

There was the crack of a rifle and wood splintered from the tree just above her head. He hadn't missed by much. Teagan pushed her to the ground and covered her body with his.

"I got him!" came a shout.

"Thank you, God," she whispered. She panicked for a minute as Teagan's weight trapped her. Then she took a deep breath. He didn't have all his weight on her. In fact, his lower half wasn't on her and his top half was supported by his elbows. He was gazing at her.

"You're not hurt, are you? I pushed you down rather roughly."

"I'm—I'm fine. I thought for a moment you were hit. Are they going to take him to the sheriff?"

He rolled on to his back before he sat up. She sat beside him. "He's dead, honey."

"How do you know?"

"He'd be yelling his head off if he were alive. Let's get you home."

He took her hand and helped her up, but when they were on their feet, he didn't let go. She felt the spark between them the whole walk home. He offered to carry her a few times, but she declined. He made her feel safe and… dare she think… loved?

CHAPTER NINE

*G*emma withdrew into herself, and Teagan didn't know what to do. It was almost as though she didn't hear him. He'd explained numerous times why he didn't just go barreling into town after Victor Lyons. He was half afraid she'd go by herself, so the next day he kept an eye on her. He wasn't sure if the sheriff was involved in the whole shady business, and until he knew he wasn't about to tell the sheriff that Richard was dead.

His brothers all agreed with him, and they were trying to figure out a plan. They needed to somehow get the banker to implicate himself in front of the sheriff. Then they would watch for the sheriff's reaction. They just needed the right plan and the right time.

He thought about Richard's claim of the gold being on the land, but he couldn't picture Mr. Maguire as a stagecoach robber. The man had been a hard worker, and frankly there hadn't been time for him to be going traipsing off after stage-coaches. Somehow, Richard had the wrong man. But Richard was dead so he couldn't be questioned. Gemma knew something she wasn't telling him, and that bothered him a lot. He wanted to take her on a picnic so they could be alone and talk, but there is still danger out there. So, he asked Dolly to fix him a lunch for two. Then he asked his brothers to eat at the bunkhouse. He didn't miss Brogan's scowl. He wondered about it, but nothing made sense. The lunch was sitting on the table which was nicely set with flowers in the middle. Teagan called out to Gemma to let her know it was time to eat and then waited.

He heard her footsteps on the stairs and went to meet her. Her beauty took his breath away as it always did. He just hated to admit it. He smiled. "Looks like it's just you and me for lunch. He didn't miss her quick frown, but he pretended he didn't see it. He gestured for her to go in front of him and followed her into the kitchen. He pulled out her chair and got her settled.

"All right, what's wrong?"

Teagan sat down and grinned. "Why would anything be wrong? I think lunch looks delicious."

Gemma shook her head. "Usually we're fighting for a place to sit and now there's only the two of us. I just find it strange is all. Spit it out. What do you want to talk to me about?"

He blinked at her and then stared for a second. "So, I take it you're not hungry."

"I'd rather we talk about whatever you want to talk about and get it over with. Then hopefully I'll be able to eat. Frankly, you make me nervous."

So, it would be a direct approach. "I remember you saying something had come between your parents, and I got the feeling that's why your father wanted me dead. I think I need to know the whole story so I can figure out what the heck is going on around here."

"I promised my mother I'd never speak of it, but you're right it's time everyone knew the truth. My mother told me she had a son with your father. My father was so enraged he took the newborn baby, rode to your ranch, and handed the boy to your father. My mother was so distraught, she never got over it. From what I understand, your mother was beyond livid. She didn't want to raise another woman's child. My mother said that her arms felt so empty. Even after she had me, her heart was still broken, and she felt as though she didn't give me enough love. I know at one point our parents were best of friends and why your father and my mother strayed from their marriages, I have no idea. But it led to my father training his rifle on your head if I said yes to your proposal."

Teagan didn't know what to say. It simply couldn't be true. He never remembered a brother magically appearing. He couldn't even begin to guess which one it might be. Gemma must've heard something wrong or her mother had lied to her.

"Why would your mother say such a thing?"

Tears filled Gemma's eyes. "Because she was dying, and she wanted me to know the truth. I also think she was afraid I might pick another Kavanagh to marry. She didn't want me picking my brother, I suppose." She stared at him, and he felt the heat of her stare all the way to his soul.

"I'm trying to think and remember, and I don't recall anyone ever saying a thing about your mother and my father. There'd be times when I thought there was something wrong between my parents. but that happens in all marriages, or at least I thought so." He scrubbed a hand down his face. "What man rips the baby out of his mother's arms and drops that child off at the father's house? I—Did my mother even know? The only thing that makes sense is the reason that you didn't marry me. I finally believe your father had a gun pointed at my head. So many lies and none of it fair to you or me. We'd have been married with children by now, I suspect. Why in the world did your father allow me to court you?"

"I begged him to tell me. I pleaded and cried but he refused to say. I hated him for the longest time. I loved you with everything inside me and I literally thought I would die without you." She lowered her voice to a stricken whisper. "It was as if you were dead, I grieved so. I never looked at another man until I had no choice. We both know what a bad choice that was." She gave her head a shake as if to dispel her thoughts. "I remember that the days we courted were the happiest of my life. But that happiness made it even harder to accept I couldn't have you. I was so afraid you would come and confront my father, and I was so afraid you wouldn't bother to fight for me. He taunted me with your absence. I kept wondering what I'd done wrong, why you never came for an answer why I said no. I kept telling myself that if I were in your shoes, I wouldn't have stopped until I got an answer. But I never heard from you again." She stood and looked out the window. Her shoulders began to shake as she sobbed.

Teagan was out of his chair in an instant. He turned her around and drew her into his arms holding her against him. He'd never thought about her suffering. He'd had no reason to think she *was* suffering. After all, she was the one who had said no. She had suffered just as he had... if not perhaps more. At least he had received the support and under-standing from his family. It sounded like she had been alone with no one to talk to. He stroked her back up and down as she sobbed deeply. His eyes misted because of the pain she was in. He'd grieved their relationship long ago, though it still hurt.

"It'll be just fine," he murmured. "I'm sorry for what you've been through, Gemma but you'll never be alone again." She stopped sobbing, and he was relieved. "I'll find you a widower, and I won't stop until I find the right one."

Gemma shook her head and she pulled away. "Gee thank you, you've always been more than helpful." She swatted him on his shoulder.

"So, the widowers can breathe easy now that you're not on the hunt?" Teagan chuckled. He put his finger under her chin and tilted her head back so he could kiss her. It was a short kiss; he didn't want to scare her off, but her eyes widened just the same.

"I think the first thing we need to do is figure out who Richard thought my father was. Why did he think he was a stage robber? And why was he so sure there was gold on the property?"

Teagan nodded. "I agree. Let's find the answers to those questions first, then if we want, we can figure out which brother isn't mine."

Gemma put her hand on his arm. "Oh, but he is your brother, he's your father's son, but he is also my brother. I think we need to weigh what it will do to this person if he finds out. What difference does it really make now? Well except for the fact that they would inherit my ranch, but I don't know if I can ever live there again anyway."

"I think you're right, honey. We need to think long and hard about this before we say a word. So, ready to eat?"

"Actually, I think I *can* eat. I feel more relieved now that you know. It's been an awful big burden of a secret to keep." She sniffed and stood straighter. "Maybe we can start a list of any times we can remember my father being gone and then find out if there were any stagecoaches robbed at those times. It won't be a long list, though. Richard never talked about having any evidence, but he must've had something to convince the bank owner to go along with him. And there's still the question of the sheriff."

They started making a list, and Teagan realized there would be a lot of traveling involved. He couldn't stay away from the ranch that long.

"Maybe we can make inquiries by telegraph?"

Teagan shook his head. "No, the sheriff would be sure to find out. I have an army friend I can trust to look into this. I'll telegram him just tell him I need him."

"What about Richard's body? Do you think he'll be found by whoever else is involved?"

"He's buried at his campsite." He stared into her eyes and smiled. "You're a survivor. You amaze me, you just do. You're bright and capable, and I'm telling this to the most beautiful woman I've ever seen. What would you say about you and me?"

"Oh, you mean while we're investigating?"

His smile broadened. "No, actually I mean I want us to get to know each other again. I want another chance without interference. I want what we should have had. That is… if you're willing?"

She turned the most beautiful crimson color. "You remember I don't like to be touched, don't you?"

"I'm not worried about it." A tender smile lit his face. "I don't think you realize how many times I've touched you in the last two days and you've been fine. Just give it some time. Let's give us a chance."

She began to wring her hands as her brow furrowed. She stared down at her hands and finally she stilled them, looked at him, and nodded. "I would like that. I would like that very much. Are we going to tell your brothers?"

Teagan grinned. "Not on your life. They'll tease us and never let us have a moment of peace. They can guess or think whatever they want. That should keep them busy and out of our way. I enjoyed having lunch with you, but I need to have one of the men go into town to send a telegram." He paused, holding her gaze with his. "I have to admit, it went better than I thought it would. Things used to be so easy between us and that's what I'm hoping for again."

"I see Dolly is out doing the wash. I'm going to go help her. Bless her for doing so much around here."

"She is a wonder." He gave Gemma a quick kiss on the cheek and left before she could say a thing.

GEMMA HUNG the clothes on the line. Telling Teagan had lightened her burdens. If only she knew which brother or maybe it was better not to know. He may not want her as his sister, or it might be awkward knowing he was born out of infidelity. How long had the affair gone on? Their actions ruined their marriages and now there was a possibility of ruining more lives.

For what seemed to be the hundredth time, she touched her cheek where Teagan had kissed her. If she wasn't so afraid, she'd be on top of the world. He'd be gentle of course, but what if she just couldn't? It wouldn't be fair to him.

A horse galloped toward the house with John Junior hanging on for dear life. Gemma abandoned the laundry and raced to him.

"What happened?" She didn't like the wild look in his eyes.

"You have to come Miss. Gemma, you have to. There's so much blood it's everywhere. Pa is hurt bad, and Lorna told me to come get you." The poor boy was shaking.

One of the hands quickly saddled up another horse for her. "Here you go Miss. Gemma. I figure you and the little boy can ride double. His horse is too lathered to go on. I'll let the boys know what's going on."

Gemma nodded as the hand helped her up into the saddle

and then handed John Junior to her. She kicked the sides of her horse and was off. It seemed like a much longer ride than she remembered. John Junior was crying, so she didn't ask him any questions.

As they approach the house, she saw blood by the wood chopping block. She slid down off the horse and then reached up for John Junior. The minute his feet were solidly on the ground, she flew to the door and opened it. The metallic smell of blood permeated the air. Aubrey and Martin were huddled in one corner while Lorna was frantically trying to stop the bleeding.

Gemma instantly put on water to heat and grabbed all the towels and sheets she could find. She went to the bed and found it saturated with blood. Gently she lifted the towel that covered his leg and looked. It was hard to tell how bad it was because of all the blood.

"John Junior, I need you to get me a bucket of water, hurry now."

Lorna was as white as a sheet. "Lorna, why don't you grab a chair and bring it over here so you can sit down. You look like you might fall over. I can tell you've taken good care of your pa already."

John Junior ran in with the bucket of water and set it down next to Gemma. Gemma took one cloth and wet it. She then washed John's leg. She sighed in relief it wasn't as bad as she thought. "John? John can you hear me?"

"Lorna, do you know if you have any whiskey in the house?"

She climbed off the chair, seeming grateful to be moving. "Yes, yes, I do. I'll get it for you."

Gemma touched John's forehead to check for fever. So far it seemed fine, but she didn't expect it to stay that way for long. She took the bottle of whiskey Lorna handed to her, opened it, and poured it over the wide wound. John groaned aloud, but he didn't open his eyes. She was thankful he was still out. She needed to stitch him up and it was going to take a bit of time.

Lorna found her some needle and thread. Gemma had her put them in the hot water for a few moments. Then she suggested that Lorna change her dress and take the children outside.

As soon as she was alone, she got the needle and thread ready and began the long process of stitching up John's leg. He'd be off his feet for a while, and the family would need some help. She shook her head, that help would probably be her. She couldn't imagine how frightened the children had been when they'd seen all the blood.

After she stitched his leg, she bandaged it and then moved him to the other side of the bed where it was clean. She had a lot of scrubbing to do, and she got to it. The door burst open, and Teagan strode inside.

"Is John all right?" Teagan walked closer and stared at John's bandaged leg. "What happened?"

"As far as I can tell he cut himself chopping wood. It could've been much worse. These kids will need a lot of help in the next few weeks. But first things first, I need you to help me change his sheets."

Teagan nodded and then assisted her in moving John so she could remove the blood-soaked sheets and replace them with clean ones. Next, he helped her scrub the floor and then gather all the towels and cloths that were bloodied.

"I don't think those are going to come clean."

"I'll just bury them in the woods."

"Teagan, I'll be staying here for the next couple weeks. There's just no other option."

"Then I'm staying too."

She widened her eyes and stared at him. "Oh no you're not. People will talk."

"They talk already so what do we care? Listen Gemma you can't do this all alone. Who's going to watch the children while you work the ranch? I know you're capable of doing all the ranch work—that's not the problem. The problem is you may be too tired to take care of the children too."

"I suppose you're right, though I do hate to admit it. You'll sleep in the barn, of course."

Teagan laughed. "Yes, I'll sleep in the barn."

"I'll start some supper. Why don't you ask Lorna where the extra blankets are? Then I suppose we need to look and see what other chores need to be done. And, Teagan... I'm glad you're staying."

A smile warmed his eyes. "Me too." Then he was gone.

Gemma bowed her head. *Thank You, Lord. This could have been much worse. Thank You for giving me the knowledge to help John. And thank You for sending Teagan. Amen*

There was enough in the house for her to make venison stew. She also made dough for a couple loaves of bread. She'd show Lorna how to bake them when she came in. Looking around, she found dried apples and decided the kids needed a treat. She got everything ready to make an apple pie, and then she called Lorna inside.

Lorna first checked on her father and then she came and hugged Gemma. "I was so scared."

Gemma hugged her back and then let go. "I don't blame you. I would have been too. Teagan and I are staying for a few days to help out. Now, how would you like to learn how to make an apple pie?"

"I'd love to learn. I tried to make biscuits many times, but no one ate them. Maybe you could teach me how to make those again."

"I think I'll be able to teach you quite a few things while I'm here. How has John Junior been doing with helping you?"

"He's been really good about doing his share of the chores. And I'm not as short tempered or tired each day."

"I'm glad to hear it." The sound of hoofbeats came from outside. Quickly she washed her hands and opened the door. Relief washed over her at the sight of Quinn sitting tall in his saddle.

"Howdy. I just saw Teagan and he told me you two are staying here for a bit. What would you like me to fetch for you? I'll have Dolly pack your bag."

"Just tell her the usual stuff. Oh, and I'd like to have the Bible that's next to my bed please."

He tipped his hat and smiled. "Will do. Someone will be by later to drop your stuff off."

He was gone before she could say thank you.

TEAGAN WASN'T sure whether he was appalled or entertained by the children at supper. Table manners obviously weren't a priority. Aubrey cried half the time while Martin decided he wanted to run around the table instead of sitting down and eating. Lorna looked like she was going to cry because no one would listen to her, and Gemma seemed to be enjoying herself.

"So, Martin, you don't like pie?" she asked casually.

Martin came to a dead stop. "Pie?"

"Yes, pie. Children that behave will get a slice of pie. You haven't been behaving."

Martin hung his head and then slowly walked to his chair and sat down. "If I'm good now, can I have some pie?"

"We'll see," Lorna replied.

Teagan shared an amused smile with Gemma. She was very good with children. Too bad she was so set on having none of her own.

He watched as she put the children to bed, giving them each a big hug and kiss. She even sang to little Aubrey. If it hadn't been for the groans of pain from John, Teagan could have closed his eyes and pretended Gemma was his wife and this was his family. But she wasn't and they weren't. He started the dishes.

Gemma sat with John, comforting him while she checked his wound. He seemed awkward by her attention. He repeatedly thanked her, both of them actually.

Teagan went over to keep him company for a bit, and John kept apologizing.

"Neighbors used to look after one another before the war. We'll need to remember to do it now," said Teagan. "This far from town, there aren't as many of us. I'll be staying in the barn. I'll check with you in the morning to see what needs to be done."

"Too much. My wife had enough to do with the children, but she tried her best, God love her. My cattle multiplied, and I have plenty of water, and thankfully the grass has been plentiful this year. I just can't round them all up and brand them and all the other things I need to do. I have no way to drive them to market either."

"You're probably sitting on a lot of money. We can give you a hand and we'll include your cattle in our cattle drive."

Moisture covered his eyes. "I don't rightly know what to say. I'll take you up on your offer. I'd hate to think of the banker getting my land. It would leave us penniless."

Teagan glanced at Gemma, who met his eyes and formed an O with her mouth. Teagan looked back at John and smiled. "Don't you worry. You just get better."

John's eyelids began to flutter closed. Teagan got up from the chair and joined Gemma by the fire. "How much do you want to bet that the banker thinks there is gold buried on this land?"

There was a twinkle in her eye. "I'll bet all the money my father stole," she smiled. "Now I won't have to wonder anymore. Darn that Richard. I feel awful I even had an inkling of doubt about my father."

Teagan reached over and squeezed her hand and let it go. "We all doubt the ones we love at some point, even if it's whether they added salt to the meal. Your doubt was a little bigger, but it made sense Richard thought that. Someone had him believing it too." He stretched. "Well, if all is set in here, I think I'll head out to the barn. You have a very generous nature. I watched it all day. Good night." He stood and went to the door. "Be sure to lock up after I close the door."

"I will."

As he lay in the hayloft, his mind was consumed with Gemma. Her patience with the children, her enjoyment of them, her comfort for John, and her smiles for him. She was really quite a woman.

CHAPTER TEN

*T*eagan stopped in for breakfast and couldn't keep his lips from twitching. The boys were asking her question after question before she even had a chance to answer. Gemma was busy with them and making breakfast while Lorna got Aubrey dressed. John looked very pale, but he was alert and watching Gemma. Teagan wished John would watch someone else. But that would not happen anytime soon.

Quinn was due at any time. He was bringing some men to help get John's ranch into shape.

"Can I get you some coffee?" Gemma asked.

"That would be nice, thank you." He watched as she poured the dark steaming liquid, humming some tune the whole while. She was happier here, and that stung. They shared a smile when she handed the coffee to him, but the boys fired off more questions.

"What's on your schedule for the day?" she asked.

"Some of the men are coming by. You?"

"Besides the obvious, I'm going to tackle the laundry. I'm

hoping to get some baking in too. I'm thinking about making cinnamon bread and cookies as well."

"Cookies?" Martin jumped up and down. "Clark, did you hear? Cookies!"

The younger boy nodded and jumped up and down with Martin.

"Will you teach me?" Lorna asked.

"Of course. We'll tackle it during naptime so we can concentrate."

Lorna smiled. "Do you know how to sew? I'm making a shirt for my pa. It's a surprise," she whispered.

"I'd love to help. How far along are you with it?"

Lorna scrunched up her forehead. "I was doing fine until I realized that one side was bigger than the other. I thought to add material to one sleeve and one of the front panels. I'm not sure the buttonholes line up either."

"No problem. That's what scissors are for, cutting out the stitches to redo it."

"I bet you never have to cut out stitches," Lorna said.

"I sure have. Many times, in fact. Once I forgot about buttons and buttonholes but then I figured my pa could just slip it over his head only the neck hole wasn't big enough. He tried not to laugh, but I ended up in tears anyway." Gemma and Lorna shared a smile that grew into a loud chuckle.

Teagan couldn't take his gaze from Gemma. Had she always been so enchanting without even trying? The sound of horses interrupted his musings. He glanced at John and still didn't like the way the man was watching Gemma. John had all day to watch Gemma and Gemma had all day to talk to John.

Teagan stood strapped on his gun belt, picked up his hat, and kissed Gemma on the cheek before he grabbed his saddlebags and rifle. "Have a good day." He didn't look back to see Gemma's reaction.

"IS HE YOUR BEAU?" Lorna asked.

"No, he's not. We're just good friends." She glanced over at John, who gave her an inquiring look, but she just smiled and shifted her gaze. She wasn't about to answer any more questions about Teagan and her.

She grabbed fresh bandages and clean water and then she sat next to John on his bed. "How are you feeling today?" She put her hand on his head and smiled before she sat back. "No fever that's always a good sign." She took off his bandages, cleaned the wound, and then replaced the bandages with clean cloths. Her face heated as John continued to stare at her. "You didn't answer. How are you feeling?"

"I'm feeling lucky and feeling blessed. Other than that, my leg hurts something awful but it could have been worse, much worse."

She didn't know what else to say, so she patted his hand, stood, and picked up the water and the soiled bandages. "Do you think you'll be all right in here if I go outside and do the wash?"

"I should be just fine, and if the little ones get in your way, just send them in to me."

Gemma and Lorna got busy gathering the laundry. There was so much of it, but she supposed that was normal for a family that size. Lorna was doing her best. She hustled everybody outside into the fresh air. John Junior helped her drag the big washtub from the barn. They put it near the water pump to make it easier for them.

She made a fire and hung a bucket of water above it. As soon as it came to a boil, she poured the water into the washtub along with some lye soap. She put more water on to boil while she washed the first few clothes against the washboard. Lorna was watching every little detail, and Gemma explained as much as she could to her. After cleaning a garment against the washboard, she put it into another washtub they had cold water in. They continued changing out the hot water once in a while until the clothes were washed.

Next, they took the clothes one by one out of the cold water and wrung them as dry as possible. After that, they were put into a basket ready to be hung up on the clothesline. She saved the dirty diapers for last and used extra soap to make sure they got clean. Meanwhile, the boys ran around with Aubrey until they all looked like they are ready to drop.

"Clark, Martin, and Aubrey, why didn't you go on inside and spend some time with your father? John Junior, be sure they don't tire your father."

"I'll go into make sure there's no trouble," John Junior said.

Gemma nodded as she and Lorna took the clean laundry over to the clothesline. Gemma's back ached, but she still needed to get all the sheets washed. Sweat ran from her forehead as the sun beat down on her. She stared up at the cloudless sky fighting a wave of dizziness. "I think we will do the sheets tomorrow."

"Good, now you have more time to show me how to bake."

Gemma smiled. "I think we'll have a little rest first before we dive into baking. But we can go over the recipes together."

Lorna smiled happily as they put their supplies away and then went inside. Gemma covered her mouth so as not to laugh when she saw the four other children all asleep with John on his bed. She put a finger to her lips, and Lorna nodded.

Gemma poured them both a cup of water, grabbed a box of recipes she'd found, and they went back outside and sat on the porch steps. They went through many before they decided on sugar cookies and the cinnamon bread. Lorna seemed more confident and not as frayed. They sat outside for a bit resting before they went back in. They sliced up bread and cheese for everyone to have for lunch and set it on the table with a towel over it to keep the flies off.

The children woke one by one and ate while Gemma and Lorna baked. Lorna enjoyed it until the house became too hot. The perils of a Texas summer, heat, flies, and mosquitoes. John Junior watched over the children and tended to his father while Gemma explained the concept of canning and preserving food for the winter.

Come next spring, I'll stop by and help you plant your garden. It takes a lot of work, but there's a great feeling when you eat food you grew yourself. Your ma must have planned ahead. I see many jars in the root cellar for this winter already. In a few weeks, we can go berry picking and then make jam and berry pies.

Teagan came in, all sweaty and dusty. He looked around and went back outside.

"What was that all about?" John asked.

"There isn't a water pump inside for him to clean up at so he's washing outside."

John looked thoughtful as he nodded.

Teagan came back in looking much cleaner. "It smells wonderful in here. I bet Lorna's been busy!"

"She sure has, and I'm sure you saw all the laundry drying outside."

Teagan nodded as he gazed at Gemma. "It must have taken most of the day."

"We've been busy. Supper will be ready soon. Why don't you fill John in on your day?"

TEAGAN ENJOYED TALKING TO JOHN, but he did not enjoy how much John watched Gemma. In fact, the more the night went on the more annoyed he got. John praised Gemma for her help and her cooking and how much she was teaching Lorna. It looked as though Gemma was lapping it up.

Didn't John realize that Gemma was only here for the children, not for him? Teagan was sure he'd made his claim by kissing her on the cheek. Either John was a bit thick in the head, or he was purposely trying to get on Gemma's good side.

After supper, Gemma helped Lorna with her sewing project. "You know so much for your age, Lorna. You are an amazing young lady."

Lorna smiled brightly while Aubrey toddled over to Gemma and wanted to be picked up. The little girl snuggled against Gemma, and Gemma looked to be in heaven. John did have an edge; he had his children. Even Clark and Martin vied for her attention. John Junior stared at her as if in love. What Teagan wouldn't give for a good old-fashioned fight with one of his brothers.

Sure, Gemma was beautiful and sweet and loving, but they didn't need to take it all for themselves. They could at least share her. Teagan sat up straight in his chair. He was jealous and selfish. He wanted Gemma all to himself, but she didn't feel that way about him. She didn't plan to make a life with him. He'd lost her, and he hadn't realized it. He'd have to get someone else to stay. He couldn't take seeing them together, all of them together anymore.

He stood and grabbed his hat. "I need to check on my horse's front right shoe. I'll turn in after that. Good night."

He left without one look at Gemma. He thought he was protecting his heart, but as he crossed the yard to the barn, he ended up feeling mean and not so proud of himself.

There was nothing wrong with his horse. He sat outside

looking up at the stars. Life had certainly been anything but boring. Helping John Dew and his children had put a lot of plans aside. He still needed to confront Victor Lyons. The longer he thought about it, he seemed to recall a tale about a shipment of army gold going missing. Was that what they'd been after? Had someone said it was buried around here? He had never believed the story, but maybe it was true. Heck, he just wanted to go home and have a shot of whiskey.

He'd leave at first light and send someone in his place. If his horse was gone, Gemma wouldn't worry. He'd leave a note, but he had nothing to write with. What was he going to do if Gemma married John? She'd said no widowers, but that was before John was injured. Now she'd had a real chance to get to know the man. She could explain to him how she didn't want to be touched. He looked like an understanding man.

He'd been in this place with Gemma before, and his heart hurt just as much the second time. He'd have to find a way to get Gemma out of his heart for good this time.

CHAPTER ELEVEN

*T*he barn was empty. She'd a feeling when Teagan hadn't shown up for breakfast that he was gone. Her heart dropped. She must be the stupidest woman in all of Texas. She never got it right. Here, she'd thought Teagan was coming to love her but as soon as he saw that John was a nice man, he left her. She'd had hopes and dreams tied up with him. Once again, she'd pictured what their children would look like because she was certain that one day, they'd be able to have them, that she'd be able to allow him to touch her. He had said he'd take the time and be patient. She'd actually believed it was possible for her to have a normal life.

Of one thing she was certain. She couldn't marry John. She saw the error in her thinking. She liked him well enough, but she didn't love him, and marriage was for a lifetime. His children could be hers, but love was something she craved. The love of a husband. She wouldn't worry about where she'd go from here, she still had her home. All she really needed was a horse and maybe a dog. A dog would be good, though she liked cats. Maybe she could let some cats live in her barn. None of it would fill the hole Teagan had left in her heart, though.

A FEW NIGHTS LATER, Gemma sat reading Teagan's Bible. Sighing, she touched the leather cover with the Kavanagh name imprinted on it. She opened it at the beginning for a change and saw the list of Kavanagh births through the generations. She traced Teagan's name and touched Quinn's when she came to Brogan's someone had glued a strip of paper over the original entry and written Brogan's name.

She sat back in the chair and closed her eyes. Brogan was her brother. He favored the Kavanaghs so no one would think otherwise. What had really happened back then? Had Mr. Kavanagh demanded his child or had her father truly demanded the baby be out from under his roof?

From the way her mother explained it, her father had gone to the Kavanagh house with the baby. What a mess! One woman whose heart broke when her child was taken and the other woman broken that she had to raise a child who wasn't hers. Oh, Mama, what were you thinking? Someone must have talked about it. When she was in school, some children weren't allowed to play with her, but that hadn't mattered to her. She was more of a tomboy. Still, it had been a puzzle. Could that be the reason the funeral had been sparsely attended? A sudden thought sent ice through her veins. Did Brogan know? He was very hostile toward her, but that didn't necessarily mean anything.

Now she knew. Should she tell Teagan or keep it to herself? Brogan had a right to the ranch, but she didn't care about that. Maybe Teagan's mother didn't have any love for Brogan just like her own mother didn't have any love left for her. So sad. Did Dolly know? She wished she didn't know. It had suddenly become a burden to carry.

If Brogan didn't know, didn't he have a right to know? If he didn't know, did she have the right to upend his world? Maybe not. No, she'd sit on the information for a while. Telling Brogan would only give him another reason not to like her.

The next morning, she was surprised to see a wagon approaching the house. She wiped her hands and took off her apron to greet whoever it was. She recognized Teagan straight off, but she stiffened as she saw the pretty woman at his side.

She'd need to brace herself, and if only she'd known she could have prepared instead of suffering from the shock that went through her. He'd found a new woman awfully quick. She would not take his bait or give him the satisfaction of jealousy, though.

She smiled and waved. "Good morning, Teagan. Who have you brought for a visit this fine day?"

Teagan smiled as he got down from the wagon. He went to the other side of the wagon and helped the pretty dark-haired woman down. "Gemma, this is Lottie. She needs a job, and I suggested she might enjoy this one. That is, if you haven't decided to stay."

Lottie's eyes widened. Teagan probably hadn't told her she might not get the job.

"It's very nice to meet you, Lottie," Gemma said carefully.

Teagan climbed back up onto the wagon. "I have work to do. I'll be back for supper."

"Have a good day, Teagan!" Lottie beamed at him as she waved.

"Let's go on in. I'll introduce you to the Dew family." Gemma led the way inside. "This is Miss. Lottie. She is here to take care of you."

"No!" Martin yelled as he ran and took Gemma's hand. Aubrey began to cry, but before Gemma could get to her, Lottie picked her up and bounced her.

Soon Aubrey smiled. "Mama?"

"I'm John Dew, Miss. Lottie. Would you mind if I talked to Miss. Gemma alone?"

"No, of course not. Children, why don't you show me around outside?" Lottie helped them all to file out.

"I didn't know anyone was coming, John. I guess Lottie needs the job, but if she's not to your liking, I'll stay until you're healed."

He nodded and gave her a wistful glance. "You wouldn't think to stay beyond that?"

"My heart was taken when I was still young, and it hasn't changed. I love the same man I've loved all my life. I wouldn't have made a good wife, John." She cleared her throat. "I—my —the man I married mistreated me, and now I don't like to be touched. I thought a widower father wouldn't want that part of a marriage since he already had children. I've recently concluded that a marriage should be filled with affection at least. I love your children, John, but I can't picture you and me together."

"I thought that was the way of things, but I had to be sure before I let go of you. There is much love and sweetness in you, Gemma." He smiled widely. "Teagan is a lucky man."

"No, Teagan and I are only friends."

His smile widened and he shook his head. "Open your heart back up to him. I think you'll find a love you never imagined possible. Lottie looks nice enough. Tell you what, if she turns out to be a shrew, I'll send John Junior to get you."

"It's going to be hard to leave, but I understand what you're saying. I need to give Teagan a chance if I can."

"Did Lottie say where she was from or how she came to need a job?"

Gemma laughed. "I only met her a minute before you did. You'll get your chance to ask questions."

"I guess that's true enough. I thank you for all you've done. Lorna is a different girl and John Junior has taken responsibility upon his shoulders. You did that. Thank you."

"My pleasure. I'd best go get the rest. It's only polite to offer Lottie a cup of coffee before we show her all that needs to be done."

IT HAD BEEN hard to keep his mind on ranching all day. What was Gemma doing? How was Lottie getting on? Did they like her enough to allow Gemma to go home with him? Lottie had been a mail-order bride who'd never became a bride. Her groom had died, and she hadn't known it until she stepped off the stage. Luckily, Teagan had been in town yesterday.

He'd had a devil of a time keeping his brothers away from her. She was comely. She was interested right away when he told her John's story. He'd also confided to her he wanted Gemma back. She agreed to help if she could. He took his hat off, ran his fingers through his hair, and then jammed his hat on again.

Would she be willing to go home with him or would he have to drive the wagon home alone? They needed to talk. Every time he thought he was getting close to her, they sprung apart. Too many secrets. He was waiting on a telegram, but he was almost positive her father had nothing to do with any gold. People swore it was stolen in Wilkes County, Georgia, that the wagon train was bushwhacked. If her father *had* stolen it, he'd never come home from the war. It wasn't on Gemma's property. He was sure her father was dead.

Her ranch was ready to go. She'd need to hire on a few men, and he already had those men working the ranch, but she needed to think it was her decision. That stubborn, loveable woman would drive him crazy.

He pulled up to the house. Would he have to talk Gemma into leaving? Would she refuse to go with him? He hadn't thought about what to do with Lottie if this plan didn't work out. Gemma was always in his thoughts. He needed to be strong and not allow the past to ruin their future. Would she tell him she didn't love him as she had done before the war? It was quite the story about having a brother who was her brother too. Could they get past that?

Their families had gotten along well enough until his father died. Then Gemma's father came and went into the office with his mother. There was a lot of yelling, and he shooed everyone outside so they wouldn't hear. He remembered he couldn't find Brogan and then Mr. Maguire slammed out of the house screaming that nothing was going to change. Now he remembered seeing Brogan still inside. His brother had been upset, but he didn't go to see Mother as he usually did, he grabbed his coat and walked out the back door.

Teagan wasn't mature enough to think of going after him. But then again, he had no idea what his mother and Gemma's father had quarreled about. Could it be Brogan? He was the most volatile of the Kavanagh brothers, and if Teagan had to pick one brother who, he thought might end up in jail he'd pick Brogan.

He wrapped the lines around the brake and climbed down off the wagon. First things first, he needed to see Gemma.

To his surprise, Gemma came outside carrying her bag. "Ready to go, Teagan? You look so surprised!" She smiled happily.

"I wasn't sure," he said in a low voice.

"I've had a lot of time to think since you left me here alone. I wouldn't be able to abide John's touch. He's a very nice man, but I will need love too. I'm not sure it will ever happen for me. We live where the largest population nearby thinks badly of me. Not all but enough to dissuade a good man." She averted her gaze. "I have land and that could be a draw, but frankly I'm not up to having a man touch me just so I can see if I can stand it. Maybe one day you or your brothers will have children, and I can be an honorary aunt to them or something."

He hated the sadness in her voice. It tore at his heart, but he was afraid she'd reject him if he asked her to marry him. He took the bag from her and put it into the back of the wagon. Then he approached her slowly while staring into her eyes. Did she care for him? He couldn't think about it. He leaned down and put his hands on her waist and helped her onto the wagon.

He jumped up onto his side and they started to drive off. "I'm happy you'll be home."

"Your home, Teagan, not mine. Though I'm not sure if I should lay claim to my ranch. It should probably go to my brother. I keep thinking and thinking, and I believe he knows already. Some things would make more sense if he did know."

"How'd you find out which brother it is?"

"Your family Bible. There is a line pasted over and his name was put there."

"It's Brogan, isn't it?"

Her mouth opened. "How?"

"I've had a lot of time to think about it. We were young and when I heard the yelling. I got all the boys out of the house except for Brogan. He hid. My parents yelling wasn't anything new, but this seemed more heated than ever before.

119

They barely tolerated each other after that. I heard the words 'I don't want him here.'" He shook his head slowly, sorrow for the boy who had been caught up in the unfaithfulness of his parents.

"My mother could be loving," he went on. "But looking back, she wasn't very loving to Brogan. It's a shame that children suffer like that. I didn't notice, I was busy learning how to run the ranch from as young as I can remember."

"I don't know what to do, what we *should* do. Why hasn't he said anything do you suppose?" she asked.

"I guess we keep our mouths shut. He'll say something when he's ready."

She nodded. "When I move back onto my ranch how will he feel?"

"You're going soon?"

"Yes. You have a ranch to run and so do I." She shot him a smile. "Thanks to you."

"About that. The only gold stolen that I could find out about was some Confederate gold. It was supposedly stolen in Georgia. The only way it could be on your property is if your father came back and buried it."

"He's dead."

"I'm waiting on a telegram confirming his death. I just don't know where Lyons got his information. Did Richard come here with the information, or did he already know Victor Lyons?"

"Truthfully, they never acted as though they even knew each other. And remember, Lyons is after John's land too."

"More to think on."

"We do have much to think about."

Teagan stopped the wagon under a tree and jumped to the ground. He helped Gemma down, took her hand and they sat under the tree in the splendid shade.

"I have had other things on my mind. I was so sure I'd

lose you to John. I promised myself that awful day you refused me I would never let you near me again. But I can't keep from loving you. At first, I thought I wasn't strong enough to go through it again, but the hope that you might love me back kept me going."

She turned her head away.

"Before you start worrying, we've been touching for a while now, and you never pull away anymore."

"It's different from a wedding night."

"I know it is. But I'm encouraged that you're not afraid of me. I am a patient man. I think I've proven that to you. I love you with everything in me. God help me, I tried not to love you. I tried to guard my heart, but I don't think I ever stopped loving you. I want for us to spend our lives together. I do want children."

She turned back to him. "For once the thought of making children doesn't send me into a panic. I like it when you hold my hand. I like when you lift me down from the wagon or a horse and your hands linger on my waist. Dancing with you is like a piece of heaven. Not only am I not afraid, but I enjoy you. When you kiss my cheek, I feel special and I feel loved. I feel almost free from the darkness that had been my life with Richard. I would give anything to be pure and untouched for you, but things went differently."

He cupped her cheek and gazed into her eyes. "Will you marry me, Gemma Maguire?"

Her smile had never been more lovely. "Yes, I will be proud to be your wife Teagan. I'm so happy it frightens me a bit that someone might try to take our happiness away."

He kissed her sweet lips and was pleased when she kissed him back. "Nothing will get in our way this time. I've prayed so long and hard for this to happen."

"I prayed for God to show me my path in life," she

confessed, "and I believe this is my answer. He is a great God full of understanding and love."

"We should probably head back home." Teagan said.

"Won't Dolly be happy?"

"She'll be over the moon," Teagan answered as he helped her up onto the wagon.

"Teagan, are you sure?"

He hated the uncertainty in her voice. Maybe with time, that would fade.

"I've never been so sure, Gemma."

They drew closer to the Kavanagh house and saw a buggy in front. Curious, they hurried inside to find Quinn upset and Dolly crying. Victor Lyons stood in the center of the room.

"I'm sorry, but you must be off the land by the end of the month."

Teagan turned to her. "Get someone to get the sheriff."

She nodded and ran back out.

"Well, it's always good to see you, Lyons," Teagan said as he sat down but not before he gave Dolly and Quinn warning glances. "Dolly could you bring me a cup of coffee and maybe some whiskey. It's been a long day already."

"Certainly." She hustled from the room.

"So, to what do we owe this visit, Lyons?"

"I was just telling—"

"Telling who? Whose name is on the land deed? Whose name is on all the accounts? Of course, you wouldn't talk ranch business with anyone but me." He glowered at the other man.

"I figured all you boys own the ranch."

"Not true. You and I were the only ones who knew that. You were not to talk about anything to do with my ranch with anyone else."

"I... I yes, of course." He reached into his pocket, drew out a handkerchief and wiped his forehead.

Dolly came in with a cup of coffee, a bottle of whiskey, and four glasses. He wanted to laugh at the number of glasses. Dolly must be in need of fortifying. She handed him his coffee and then sat down, glaring at Victor.

Quinn showed no reaction to the fact that the ranch was in Teagan's name.

"I thought I heard you order an eviction when I walked in?"

"Why yes, that is why I am here. You haven't paid your taxes and they are a year overdue. As you know, after a year the house and land are no longer yours."

"It doesn't make it yours either. You have nothing to do with this property. Not a penny is owed. Do you think me to be so far into my dotage that I'd forget I paid my taxes? I have the receipt, you fool. Now, what is this really all about? You went after the Maguire land, then John Dew's, and now mine. Interesting to say the least." He leaned forward, locking his gaze on the other man. "Who do you work for?"

"I have no idea what you mean!" Victor's face turned a ruddy red.

Teagan confidently opened the bottle and poured the four whiskeys. He handed the first one to Dolly. And he kept his jaw from dropping when she downed it all in one quick swallow.

"Now let's see if we have this right. Richard Parks is a family acquaintance of yours and the two of you were positive they buried the stolen Confederate gold on the Maguire land. Unless you saw the ghost of Captain Maguire, I doubt that happened. The captain is dead. I have signed statements he died right after Gettysburg. It's interesting that you would make such a mistake since you seemed to know so much about the robbery and it being in Georgia and all. You told everyone at Bobbie's Saloon your theories about the missing money."

Teagan sat back and swirled his rich amber whiskey in the glass for a moment before he drank it down. "You like to gamble, Lyons. You'll bet on anything from cards to what color petticoat a woman is wearing. And Richard kept right up with you. You even gave him a big mortgage on the house you knew he didn't own. How could he own it if he was already married to someone else? You two had such a time staying at Bobbie's Tavern every evening. But you weren't lucky and neither was Richard. The only other money in your bank safe was the taxes we all paid. I'm thinking you lost that money too and thought you'd scare a few folks and evict them and then sell their property."

Teagan saw the sheriff and Gemma quietly walk in. "I think you convinced Richard there was money buried because he dug, and he practically took the Maguire house down looking for that money. Captain Maguire never deposited anything in your bank, and you knew he must have his money somewhere. You were right, but Gemma dug it all up long ago. You put her in danger and that can't be forgiven. What I can't figure out is why come here? The Kavanagh brothers would never go quietly."

Victor Lyons helped himself to more whiskey. "I have a buyer for your place. No one wanted the other two patches of dust. Especially since the Maguire place didn't have any cattle. But on your ranch, I had a bidding war and I'm swimming in money now. So one way or another you will be leaving." He pulled out a small two-shooter and aimed it at Teagan.

As fast as the gun came out, it was shot out of his hand by Quinn. The sheriff came forward and trained his gun on the banker. "Who would have thought of the lengths you'd go?"

Lyons shrugged. "Richard ran off on me. He even sold

everything in the house. He didn't get much, but it scared the girl enough that she left."

"Richard is dead. He kidnapped Gemma and when she escaped, he pulled his gun on her. I should have told you, sheriff, but I didn't want whoever was working with Parks to know he was dead. I just can't imagine you for such a fool, Lyons."

"I owed Richard for a long while now, and somehow he found me. He threatened to kill me. It's not my fault!"

The sheriff laughed. "That's what they all say. I'll take the trash out with me." He hauled Victor up by the back of his collar and shoved him outside.

"Teagan, how did you know all that?" Gemma asked.

He held his arms out and she ran to him and snuggled against him when he wrapped her into his embrace. "I had an old friend check around for me. I was pretty sure your father never had any gold. Parks and Lyons have been in trouble with the law before."

"I'm glad you found out the truth," she said.

"Amen to that!" Dolly said.

Quinn was deadly quiet.

CHAPTER TWELVE

*I*t was pure torture to wait for Teagan to get back from his meeting with his brothers. She could imagine their concern that they didn't own any of the ranch. That was how Teagan's father had wanted it. The oldest would have control. That didn't sit well with Quinn. It never had.

Gemma tried, reading, sewing, cleaning; none of it helped. Time moved so slowly, and she prayed that the brothers would understand and accept the way of things. As far as Teagan was concerned, they all owned the ranch.

The door opened and Teagan walked in looking like he had lost his best friend. He walked to the sideboard and poured a drink and drank it down.

"What happened?"

"I don't rightly know. Everyone understood except for Quinn. He's packing his things and he plans to leave."

"For how long?"

"He doesn't know. He hasn't been happy since he came back from the war. He really loved that nurse and one day he woke and she was gone. No note, nothing. It just hurts, it feels as though Quinn blames me or that he thinks I stole the ranch. I guess he just needs time."

"We all need time now and then. He loves you, Teagan." She went to him and wrapped her arms around his middle. "*I love you, Teagan. Quinn will be back.*"

He pulled her closer and kissed the top of her head. "I love you too."

TEAGAN WAS PUTTING liniment on his horse Sandy's front leg. His heart hurt for Quinn, but it was also near bursting with love for Gemma. He needed her, she made him laugh, she made him feel loved.

"I'm going to my own ranch!"

"Brogan, what are you talking about?"

"I would never have pushed Gemma off the ranch, but since she'll be living here, I might as well claim my birthright." Brogan widened his stance and glared at Teagan. "Don't pretend you didn't know."

"Not until recently. No, I didn't know. Gemma's mother told her before she died, but she didn't say which brother. Gemma found your name in the family Bible, pasted in. It makes no difference to me. You're my brother."

"I had a right to know the minute you found out!" Brogan scowled.

"You are absolutely right, but I didn't know what to do, how to bring it up, and I'm sorry. You're still a Kavanagh. The land belongs to Gemma, but go on. I understand you need time to yourself."

Brogan shook his head. "I wanted to throttle you! Why do you have to be so understanding? You know where I'll be."

Teagan nodded. "I'll let you tell the others if you choose to. Take care of yourself out there and if you need anything

I'm here." Teagan dropped the liniment and reached out, hugging Brogan. "Don't be a stranger."

Brogan nodded and glanced away. He saddled his horse and was on his way.

Teagan felt a weight on his heart, but there wasn't a thing he could do about it. Now he had two brothers out there. He sighed. They knew how to take care of themselves.

EPILOGUE

*H*is heart squeezed as he watched Gemma walk down the aisle. She was absolutely beautiful in her lavender dress. Her smile lit up his life and he couldn't take his gaze off her. After all this time she would be his wife. It had taken more patience than he had but she willingly kissed him and held him. The happiness she gave him made it all worthwhile. He'd been upset about his brothers, but she always calmed him.

She stood next to him, and the love in her eyes humbled him. He just hoped he was always deserving of such love. She didn't mind living in the house with his brothers. If he'd been her, he'd have wanted his own house, but he needed to be in their lives, he needed to know what was going on, he couldn't lose another one. She understood.

They exchanged rings and finally she was his. He kissed her and kissed her and then he let her up for air, giving her a grin.

She smiled back and blushed. She put her arms around his neck. "I love you Teagan, with all my heart."

His eyes grew moist. "I love you too, with all that is in me."

They greeted the guests, had a meal, and cut the cake. They danced until they could sneak away.

"Where are we going?" she asked laughing.

"We're almost there." He held her hand, still reeling. She was his wife.

They climbed a hill, and he pulled her back to him and wrapped his arms around her middle. He kissed the side of her neck, and she shivered.

"What a view! You can see a lot of the ranch from here. Teagan, what do you think we will be doing in ten years?"

"Who knows what tomorrow brings? I know I love you, and that will never change. I suspect we'll have children and be very happy. God has been so very generous to us."

She nodded. "Yes, He has. I bet most of your brothers find wives and we will have a ranch full of children. It sounds like heaven to me." She was silent for a time. "Teagan, I want us to have children, and somehow you've made it so I'm not afraid anymore. I never ever thought I'd have your love again. I had the greatest of love and the most painful hurt, and now I have an even greater love. All with you. And the greater love is the best. I'm sorry neither Quinn nor Brogan came to the wedding, but they have their own lives to work out. They'll be back. They love you."

"My heart feels like it's going to explode, Gemma. This has to be the most incredible sunset I've ever witnessed."

"Me too. Let's go inside and see about making children. I'm ready and I know you won't hurt me."

"I will treasure you all of our days." He wrapped his arms around her and gave her a deep kiss. Then he offered her his arm. He was taking her home for good and nothing ever felt so good or so right. Gemma had been right; God is good.

THE END

Thank you for reading Teagan's story. If you enjoyed it, please leave a review on Amazon. It'll help me to get better advertising and hopefully it'll convince others to read it too.

Next up is Quinn's story. He's had his heart broken. How he will trust a woman even if he marries her?

ABOUT THE AUTHOR

Sexy Cowboys and the Women Who Love Them...
Finalist in the 2012 and 2015 RONE Awards.
Top Pick, Five Star Series from the Romance Review.
Kathleen Ball writes contemporary and historical western
romance with great emotion and
memorable characters. Her books are award winners and
have appeared on best sellers lists including: Amazon's Best
Seller's List, All Romance Ebooks, Bookstrand, Desert
Breeze Publishing and Secret Cravings Publishing Best
Sellers list. She is the recipient of eight Editor's Choice
Awards, and The Readers' Choice Award for Ryelee's
Cowboy.
Winner of the Lear diamond award Best Historical Novel-
Cinders' Bride
There's something about a cowboy

facebook.com/kathleenballwesternromance
twitter.com/kballauthor
instagram.com/author_kathleenball

So Many Roads to Choose

The Settlers

Greg

Juan

Scarlett

Mail Order Brides of Spring Water

Tattered Hearts

Shattered Trust

Glory's Groom

Battered Soul

Romance on the Oregon Trail

Cora's Courage

Luella's Longing

Dawn's Destiny

Terra's Trial

Candle Glow and Mistletoe

The Kabvanagh Brothers

Teagan: Cowboy Strong

Quinn's Story

The Greatest Gift

Love So Deep

Luke's Fate

Whispered Love

Love Before Midnight

I'm Forever Yours

Finn's Fortune

Glory's Groom

Made in the USA
Monee, IL
25 March 2022

93528608R00083